CALL OF THE UNDERTOW

CALL OF THE UNDERTOW

LINDA CRACKNELL

FREIGHT BOOKS

Second impression January 2014

Freight Books
49-53 Virginia Street
Glasgow, G1 1TS
www.freightbooks.co.uk

A CIP catalogue reference for this book is available from the British Library

ISBN 978-1-908754-30-1
eISBN 978-1-908754-31-8

Typeset by Freight in Garamond
Printed and bound by Bell and Bain, Glasgow

the publisher acknowledges investment from
Creative Scotland toward the publication of this book

For Phil

Linda Cracknell has published two collections of short stories, Life Drawing (Neil Wilson Publishing, 2000) and The Searching Glance (Salt, 2008). She writes drama for BBC Radio Four and edited the non-fiction anthology A Wilder Vein (Two Ravens, 2009). She received a Creative Scotland Award in 2007 for a collection of non-fiction essays in response to journeys on foot, Doubling Back (Freight, 2014). She teaches creative writing in workshops across Scotland and internationally and lives in Highland Perthshire.

ONE

When Maggie saw through the window that a snowman had appeared in her garden she put on wellies and strode out to face it, fist clenched against an impulse to punch its head off.

She prowled the garden, searching for clues in the blanket of snow that stretched the land even flatter on this bleak March day. From the trails, she could see that the intruders had rolled snow across the garden from her front gate. But she found no footsteps. She walked to the gateway and peered down the silenced lane, rutted with a single pair of tyre tracks. A newcomer still teetering on the edges of her own territory, she had no idea why anyone would sneak up on her like this.

She crept back inside and stood at one of three large windows in the sitting room, looking north to Dunnet Bay. She'd arrived two weeks ago to this place that seemed to scratch at her. Raw winds streamed past the windows carrying grains of ice or sand or both. The newspapers told of trucks lifted from harbour-sides by winter storms and smashed against walls. There was no shelter in the low-lying fields. Cattle, fenced in by flagstones processing like linear graveyards, hoisted their rumps into north-easterlies and sunk their heads. The strange abrasiveness had put her at ease; it suited her. It wasn't an unfriendly place. No one passed her on the street without a greeting, but none of them had imposed further.

She glanced at the snowman. For what was supposed to be an empty place, there was now a sense that there could be people watching her.

From the window she looked through a lattice of bare branches outlining chinks of colour beyond. The effect was like leaded stained glass. She could just make out the jagged rise and fall of the dunes and beyond them a snippet of sea darkened by the nearby snow; the surf a yellowy-pink. No one lived between her and the sea. There was just a cluster of derelict farm buildings and birds that crashed their wings about in the gaunt trees; rooks' nests perched in the dark filigree of topmost twigs.

She left the window, made coffee, and retreated to her study to settle to work. The phone jangled and she leapt to her feet.

'How is it?' she heard when she picked up the phone.

'Good grief, Richard,' she said, her breath ragged. 'Isn't it two months before you have to start harassing me about the atlas deadline?'

During the fortnight in which she'd been freelance and Richard had become her commissioning editor, he seemed to respond to her emails with phone calls, despite their habit of emailing when they'd been colleagues working at adjacent desks.

'I meant life in wolf territory,' he said.

She knew he was referring to Timothy Pont, an early map-maker they both admired who'd been Minister of Dunnet Church, not far from her new home. In the late 16th century Pont had drawn sketch maps of the whole of Scotland which informed the earliest map of the country in Joan Blaeu's monumental world atlas. Pont's maps of the north coast showed vast white spaces into which only the capillary ends of rivers dared to penetrate; where no people seemed to be. '*Extreem wildernes*' he had written across the white, and '*verie great plenty of wolves doo haunt in this desert places*'. Even now the road atlas didn't make it look so different and had seemed to summon her here. To the white spaces on the map.

'I'm surrounded by snow,' she said.

'Yikes.'

'Don't worry, there are daffodils coming up through it. Wolf territory is perfect,' she said, trying not to think about the snowman.

'Really?'

'Yes.'

Backing off as he usually did when pushed, he updated her on office politics, upcoming conferences, his most recent trips to theatres, concerts and restaurants in Oxford.

'They're paying you too much for this job, aren't they?' she said, teasing him for his promotion.

'Jealous, are we?'

That evening she locked the doors and checked the catches on windows thoroughly before going to bed. She slept like a sheepdog with one ear cocked. Her dreams were infiltrated by the still unfamiliar slips and shudders of the fridge, a rattle in a pipe, twigs cracking against a window. A wind rose up and howled around the edges of the house.

She got up early and went straight to one of the sitting room windows. The snowman had grown a luxuriant mop of dark hair. She went out, shoulders braced against an Arctic blast that grappled with her coat collar, and found the hair was fashioned from straggling lines of kelp. The snowman had grown a face too – a limpet shell for each eye, a razor shell for a long straight nose, and a curved gull feather for a smile. She stood scowling at it and then shuffled around her garden as she had the day before, head bent, hunting for tracks. She found none except her own.

She stood in her gateway to listen. Despite the cold, the birds were rioting in the trees nearby as if it was spring. Trills, cheeps, something that sounded like a mechanical clock being wound up, and a long sucking sound like a toothless great-aunt with a humbug. She had no idea which noises came from which birds. A tiny one had become familiar in recent days, calling her attention with its 'chick-chack' only to bob out of sight over the garden wall, flashing a white rear end.

Maggie's landlady, Sally, appeared walking towards her up the snow-filled lane with her two boys, heading for their large bungalow a short distance beyond Flotsam Cottage.

'Settling in okay?' Sally smiled against the wind which carved away the flesh of her face and aged her by twenty years.

'Surprised by this.' Maggie indicated the snow.

'Winter's last snarl,' Sally said. 'This time of year, just takes a puff of westerly and it's away.'

Sally wore sheepskin mitts and in each one she held the hand of one of her two boys, hats pulled down over their ears. The children remained silent, kicking at the snow, and Maggie ignored them while she exchanged a few words with Sally about the cottage.

'The boys like your snowman. Don't you?' Sally jiggled their hands.

They nodded, carried on kicking.

'I didn't... It wasn't me,' Maggie said, embarrassed at the implication that she would waste time on something so childish. She wondered briefly if it could have been these two who built it, but they seemed too disinterested somehow. 'I don't know where it came from.'

'Really?' Sally laughed. 'A welcome from a well-wisher, perhaps.'

'Perhaps,' Maggie said.

'And how's the work going?' Sally asked. 'I've really no idea what a cartographer does.'

Maggie suspected Sally didn't believe there was any work. No visitors arrived with briefcases; Maggie never went out dressed in a suit.

'I mean are you off with gadgets and all that when you go out walking?'

Maggie laughed, explaining how the places she mapped were usually the other side of the world and she never even had to visit them. 'I just like walking,' she said. 'That's not work.'

Her walks so far had taken her half a mile to the village shop, from where she'd been making ever-increasing loops back home to get to know the area, charting it with her feet in her usual way. She observed oddities: roads that seemed fiercely silent were periodically tyrannised by boy-racer exhausts; a brown-harled beauty salon stood alone by the roadside; and on still days columns of steam plumed from the centre of the village. She noticed these things and then set them aside.

Sally looked thoughtful. 'Callum's doing a map-making project at school, aren't you, love?'

The smaller of the two boys nodded.

Sally cocked her head down at Callum. 'You might get some tips from Maggie, eh?' The mother smiling at her child, cupping her hand on his head, pulling him into her side. 'Maybe I'll send you round.' Sally looked up at Maggie and winked.

'No, don't,' Maggie said, caught off-balance, her armpits

flashing with heat. The child, Callum, poked a hole in the snow with his toe. But she'd also heard her own rudeness. 'I mean, I've a lot of work on. I'm not sure I can help. Not at the moment.'

Sally tossed her head, her expression flickered briefly and then she smiled. 'Don't worry, I was only joking.' She gathered the children up. 'Well, boys, shall we go and get warm?'

They said their goodbyes. Maggie paused and turned to watch the three backs moving away from her along the lane towards their own door, half wanting to call them back and say something more friendly.

Back indoors she stood at a window glaring out at the snowman who'd ruffled her calm. She felt as if a handful of dark birds had been thrown up within her, thrashing beaks and wings against confining walls. Then they dropped to accept their earthbound trap, motionless except for the occasional blink of an eye.

TWO

Maggie had rented 'Flotsam Cottage', a single-storey steading conversion on the outskirts of the village, without viewing it. On a peninsula, practically an island, at a latitude of 58° 37' 21"N, as far north as places with ice-names like Anchorage and Stavanger, the cottage had seemed right when she found it online and she'd signed a six-month lease – a long enough horizon for her to aim for.

In the days and weeks before moving she'd kept a road atlas open on the kitchen table and looked at it while eating breakfast. A road atlas, usually castigated by people like her for reducing landscape to a driver's myopia, had been exactly right for her needs. She toured her eye around the profile of the peninsula, saw it as an animal head, perhaps a cat, with the nose raised at the north-east corner – Duncansby Head. To the south of Duncansby was the great yawning mouth of Sinclair Bay, toothless but opened wide as if in a scream, lined with a thin slice of yellow sand.

West of Duncansby was a round bear-like ear, before the back levelled away into smaller lumps and bumps towards Dunnet

Bay, a soft and vulnerable indent with its wide strip of sand, a chink in the armour of what she took to be a rocky exterior.

The place names were enjoyable to say aloud; unfamiliar and sibilant. Sibster, Staxigoe, Slickly, Sordale. They sounded foreign – Skirza, Ulbster, Ackergill – left there by the Vikings probably, though from what she'd read, the Norse history of Caithness was forgotten now, only occasionally uncovered when sands shifted from a Viking burial site. The place names marched a set of characters fit for a children's storybook into her head: Aukengill the herring; Murkle the mink; Rattar spoke for itself. The roads on the map, the blue branches of the rivers and tributaries, made lines along which characters might be drawn to each other and meet.

'You're mad,' her sister Carol said when Maggie showed her the final page of the road atlas, the expanses of blank white paper, the few wiry roads and the tiny shaded areas indicating settlements. 'Even I can read a map enough to see there's nothing there. It's not like you to be so remote.'

Instead of answering she randomly re-opened the atlas near the front; the South. Reading, Newbury, Basingstoke, Didcot, Southampton. The pages were a crazed circuit board of crossing wires - green or red for A roads, blue for motorways. Large shaded areas spoke of dense populations. Carol frowned at the atlas and Maggie closed it with a small thump; a strained line of understanding between them as usual. Carol, older by only two years at 42, even physically contradicted her sister: fair and curvy to Maggie's darkness, height, crane-like angularity.

Maggie's friend Helen was more polite. 'I've never heard of it. Apart from that place of course.' She poked a finger at John O'Groats, known as the most northerly point, even though the map clearly gave this role to Dunnet Head further to the west.

She bought a car, a second-hand Volvo.

'You're going to drive again?' Carol's tone now sweetened, sniffing her own agenda for Maggie of 'getting back' to something.

'Easiest way to get there with my things,' Maggie had said.

No one tried to stop her, but she sensed the whispered conversations, the concern. Helen offered her help with packing up. Even after Maggie had stopped attending the 'Joining In' community choir they'd both sung in, Helen and Maggie maintained their ritual of meeting for a coffee and bun at their favourite deli afterwards, the chat safely confined to weather, singing, buns. She also tried to put Maggie in touch with friends she said lived in the far north. She wasn't the only one. They handed her pieces of paper with scribbled addresses and phone numbers. But the friends were usually in Inverness, a hundred miles away, or even Perth, two hundred. They were hardly going to be neighbours.

'Does Frank know?' Carol asked.

'We're not married anymore.'

'I know,' Carol said. 'But.'

'He knows.'

She packed essentials into the car and pointed it towards that far corner of the country, teeth gritted, radio up loud, crunching indigestion tablets; the first time she'd driven in two and a half years. Pulled north and north, with her left-behind self snapping at her heels but eventually dropping back and back, out-paced and shrinking as she passed Glasgow, the junctions thinning out, the land between settlements spreading. She stopped for a break in Pitlochry in the darkening afternoon, saw a hairdresser lolling and idle in her window, went in and had her dark hair cut short there and then. She barely looked at its effect on her face in the mirror, thought of it as a point of no return. Then beyond Inverness fewer and fewer villages with chains of orange street lights glowing out of the black and her breathing steadying. A road that rolled; a dark chasm now falling away to her right and one or two solitary ships' lights out there in parallel journeys to her own.

And finally the car had brought her to rest in these flat, open lands of the peninsula where there was nothing to hide behind. You could see so far; see your enemies coming. It was a relief to be so certain of her safety. That was, until the snowman had arrived in her garden.

Just as Sally promised, salt-laden winds turned the snow to slush, disappearing the snowman overnight except for a snowball left seeping into the grass. When the clocks changed at the end of the month, it seemed no warmer but the searing skies suddenly arced into long days, awaking a sort of hum in her and calling her beyond her established circuits.

'You've been there a month and haven't made a pilgrimage to Dunnet Church yet?' Richard said at the end of a phone call one morning.

'I've walked along the beach loads,' she said. 'But it's really long. Dunnet's the very far end of it. I've got work to do for some horrible boss, remember?'

Putting down the phone, she looked out of the window and saw the cold brightness of the day. Her deadline was still weeks away. She stood up and closed the laptop, pushed her bicycle past the car where it sat abandoned at its first resting place on the gravel driveway.

She pedalled towards the village passing the sentry-box beauty salon and a now familiar copse of tall, leafless trees amidst which shimmered a boarded-up church. A bit further along was a primary school. Then the village with its grey, squat cottages laid out on a grid of streets by a man who'd invented it from a quarry in the flagstone era – hence its name, Quarrytown. She had no notion of who might live in the cottages now. There appeared to be no source of employment other than the small commercial laundry behind the hotel that gushed out steam scented with a faint memory of Maggie's grandmother. The streets often seemed empty except for tangles of boys and bicycles outside the chip shop or smokers leaning on the side wall of the hotel. Her visits to the shop had been an impersonal relief. Its window was chequered with notices for community events: a double glazing exhibition, a pipe band, some sort of crafts competition. Nothing of interest to her.

It was as if time had forgotten this place, abandoned it to the nuclear facility along the coast. And yet a new 'goldrush' of wave and tidal energy developments was promised in the Pentland Firth. Swarms of prospectors might arrive to civilise the derelict properties that punctuated the land at half-mile intervals. Perhaps it was already happening. She'd heard the relentless churning of cement-mixers as she walked around the village, seaming together the breeze-block walls of new bungalows.

She freewheeled through the trees leading from the village towards the beach, the dark tunnel briefly opening out at a derelict Lodge Cottage marking the entrance to a long-gone grand house. Then she was out into light and onto the road running parallel to the bay, walled off from it by a high line of dunes prickling with marram grass.

At the tall white church at the heart of the cottages in Dunnet a creaky woman with finger-tips almost L-shaped with arthritis was putting flowers into vases. The two of them fell into a small, echoey exchange.

'The congregation's dropped to under ten,' the woman said, peering at Maggie after she'd admired the plaque commemorating Pont's stay as Minister here. 'All aged over sixty. The structure of the building needs attention too.'

It was as if she thought Maggie could mobilise a congregation as well as a cement mixer to shore up the church. The skin around the woman's eyes was fragile, crumbling. She then enticed Maggie to climb a steep rickety ladder to the belfry where a magnificent bell hung on a wooden gantry.

'A gift from the estate of Mary Oswald after she died in 1788,' the woman called up croakily from the bottom of the ladder.

'Who was Mary Oswald?' Maggie asked.

'Owned half of Jamaica. Father-in-law was another minister here.'

Maggie descended the unstable ladder.

As if released from some sort of hibernation, from something that had been constraining her explorations, she pedalled on. After another four miles, at Dunnet Head, she walked a short way from the lighthouse and paused on the cliff top, lay down on her stomach above a great white-stained slot into which spume flowed far below.

Years before, when they'd been married, Frank had taken her several times to the west coast, near to the isles of Skye and Mull, to walk the hills. Arms of land tumbled by birch or oak woodlands sloped into the sea, and islands always gave the eye something to cling to, making the sea seem benign. This end-of-the-world suddenness wasn't what she expected from Scotland. Nevertheless the heaving swell against rocks thrilled her.

Dark birds with white bibs stood shoulder to shoulder on the ledges below her, the smell of their guano brewing a cauldron of ammonia. It was like a steeply-tiered theatre, but not a sedate one; more like the most raucous Elizabethan playhouse echoing with catcalls and drunken laughter. The birds stepped from their ledge into the abyss, a black and white swoop joining them to a web of flight paths between the cliff and the sea's surface. Then they swept up again to alight with uncanny precision, perching back amidst the crowd.

Pairs chattered into each other's ears, preening each other's heads, their necks oily and eel-like. She thought she recognised something like tenderness in their behaviour. With its long slender beak one bird nibbled at its partner's neck and under its chin. The recipient shuffled, twitching its wings impatiently like a child having its school tie straightened before it's allowed to leave the house. They prickled up a sense of her own isolation. It was almost as if these birds were more human than herself.

She heard voices. Two men with binoculars and moss green jackets came into sight. Perhaps she should get binoculars, buy a bird book, be able to give them names as she could roughly do with flowers. She recalled boring friends of her ex-husband who carried dictaphones into which they whispered the names of conquests.

Getting to her feet, she left the vantage point to the men.

She cycled back down through the village of Dunnet, headed onto the Dunes road and stopped at the 'Sandpiper Centre', a place overlooking the beach that was dedicated to birds.

'Aye, they're "oakies"', the Ranger said when she described the birds. 'That's what they get called up here.'

His accent was Scottish, but didn't sound like the voices she heard in the shop. She imagined he'd come from somewhere to the south, somewhere she'd driven through blindly.

'"Guillemots" to the rest of us,' he said, pushing square

spectacles up his nose. He'd stood up eagerly from his desk when she came in, a pale-faced man with sandy-coloured hair. The air he displaced gushed with the scent of cigarette-smoke.

'Very handsome,' Maggie said.

'Ach, thanks,' he grinned at her.

'The birds,' she said. 'The guillemots.'

'Oh aye,' he said. 'And fantastic divers. They can stay down for a couple of minutes or more. One or two get deeper than a hundred feet.'

'Are they rare?'

'No, but in serious decline. Could have heard them a mile away from that cliff ten years ago.'

'Oh?' Maggie shook her head slightly.

'Seem to be starving. Lack of sand eels.'

She started to edge away from the desk towards a huge picture-window that revealed horizontal stripes of sea, sky, and sand. Shoals of birds swooped diagonally, plaiting and separating above a sea-horizon that spread between two arms of land. The Quarrytown side was dark with its tight, singular pocket of winter-bare trees. Dunnet Head wasn't visible from here but Dwarwick Head, closer to the beach on the same peninsula, soared up golden to her right. But then as she watched the opposing headlands alternated – one darkening whilst the other illuminated, as if in some coded dialogue with each other.

'Kittiwakes are back,' the Ranger said from behind her, and then pointed to a flock of glittering white birds tumbling together from one spot to another above the waves. 'Come and see this.'

Tiredness ambushed her out of nowhere; she was sorry she'd begun the conversation. She seemed to be the only visitor to the Centre despite it being the start of April, which she thought of as springtime.

He took her to a screen, offered her a seat and leant over her to press a button. Even his shirt sleeves smelt of cigarette smoke, although she could smell mint on his breath now too, and he seemed to be chewing.

'You'll like this,' he said as the screen came to life.

She watched the sleek silhouette of a dark brown bird; a fluid line from beak to its tightly pointed tail. It seemed to be propelled by one flap of a wing, its speed apparently disproportionate to the effort.

'Right,' she said. 'They're good at flying.' Managing not to say, 'surprising for birds'.

A slight chuckling sound came from behind her, but he continued to watch the screen over her shoulder, keeping her pinned there herself. It was a little like the flights she'd watched from the cliffs, but now the birds' wings seemed to beat in slow motion. The camera panned out, took in more. The air thickened and clouded. The sounds, she realised, were more washy, not filled with the cliff-clamour she'd heard. She was drawn in, puzzled.

Then a whole flock of the birds started rushing past each other, rising and falling. They rolled or turned to avoid each other with minute flaps of their wings or twitches of their tails. They looked in profile almost like tiny turtles, and when she saw a trail of bubbles, she realised that the blue that held them was water.

'They fly underwater?'

'Brilliant, eh?' He laughed, still apparently thrilled by the sight despite its familiarity.

'Can I watch it again please?' she said.

She went back to the Centre a few days later, stood again at the window studying the view through binoculars, sipping a cup of metallic-tasting tea from the machine to warm up after the walk along the beach.

The Ranger introduced himself as Graham. Embarrassed to be the only person there again, she galloped questions at him, garrulous almost, as if making up for a long silence. Although he wasn't from the area, he seemed to know it well.

'Where is everyone?' she asked.

Occasionally she saw men in boats putting out creels or salmon nets. She'd once seen a small group of surfers far out in the bay, black and seal-like, lying on their boards but never apparently making any progress on the waves. The vast beach between the two villages was sometimes walked by people with dogs or crossed by a solitary horse rider, but they were widely spaced, would never make eye contact. There was no sense here of the 'promenade'; of people dressing up to be seen on the beach. It was a ritual reserved for the shop and, for men perhaps, the pub.

'You never see anyone much on the beach this time of year,' said Graham.

'Lovely,' Maggie said. 'The quiet, the emptiness.'

'Try working here. And not going off your rocker. That's why I stay in Helmsdale. Long way, but I've pals there.'

She wondered if Graham detected that she was an outcast and was talking to her out of kindness. She didn't like to tell him that he needn't bother.

'The job's different come high summer,' he said. 'When the caravan site's full. There's walks to lead; ground-nesting birds' eggs to protect from dogs; I might even have to defend the dunes one of these days'.

'What do you mean?'

'Some bastard's thieving the sand,' he said.

'Why?'

'Local people've probably been taking the odd sack for a couple of millennia.' Graham shrugged. 'But someone's upped the scale recently. Just see the tyre marks in the mornings. Not my job to enforce it, but still, if I lived nearer I'd get a wee vigilante group together.'

'Who're they nicking it from?' she asked.

He looked at her without an answer. It was obvious that sand couldn't really belong to anyone. Then he returned to his desk.

She was standing alone at the window with her eyes on the beach when she heard the door open. A great squabble of voices exploded in. She didn't turn.

'Primary Five,' a female voice trumpeted.

The noise immediately subsided, leaving a moment of shuffling quiet.

'That's better.'

Sweat prickled in Maggie's armpits. The room crowded in on her; suddenly airless. She heard the commanding woman greeting Graham.

'Now we've all met Graham before,' she said to her class. 'When he's been in school to help out with the wildlife garden. But not all of you have been here.'

Graham introduced the Centre, pointing out a few things that they could explore, emphasising interactive exhibits with buttons to press.

'See that fella?' His voice now projected towards the window where Maggie was trapped. 'What do you call that?'

Various children volunteered: 'Seagull.'

Maggie gathered he was pointing at a passing gull.

'If it's crossing the sea we call it a seagull. But if it's crossing the bay, we call it...'

'A bagel!' a single voice cried.

It became apparent from what he said that the class had also been visiting Dunnet Church. Without turning around Maggie waited for the school party to disperse around the room so she could make a dive for the door.

'Any questions?' Graham asked.

As an answer there was a shuffling anticipation of movement. Maggie picked up her bag.

'One minute.' Graham detained them. 'There's someone here I should introduce you to. You're very lucky in fact. This lady...'

Maggie prickled, stiff-necked. Was he referring to her?

'...Maggie Thame is a modern day Timothy Pont.'

Blood drained from her face.

'Maggie?' Graham summoned.

She took a breath and turned, her hand pressing at the familiar sting in her stomach. Twenty bright blue sweatshirts; eyes trained on her. Callum was there, Sally's youngest, and she thought she saw him nudge the boy next to him and whisper something. Elsewhere giggling huddles suggested conspiracy and made her wonder whether the snowman-builder might be amongst them. She turned her gaze away.

Graham now spoke to Maggie: 'This is Mrs Thompson, head of your local primary school. And these rascals are Primary Five.'

Maggie nodded, tried to smile.

Mrs Thompson strode towards her with an outstretched hand. She was a surprisingly tiny woman with short dark hair and a business-like satchel over one shoulder. She wore narrow, rimless glasses.

'We heard a cartographer had moved to the area.'

Maggie reacted to the word 'moved', with its permanent,

bricked-in sound. 'Well it's only...'

But Mrs Thompson boomed on over her: 'Remember that word "cartographer", children? What does it mean?'

Mumbled answers came back and then the teacher released a small explosion with, 'Okay children, off you go,' calling through the mayhem: 'And quietly. You've only got fifteen minutes'.

She turned to Maggie again. 'Very pleased to meet you. The children are doing their own maps this term, just simple things. What is it you work on yourself?'

Maggie explained about her freelance status, her current project. 'So you see, I can work from anywhere.'

'Well, lucky us.' Mrs Thompson was rummaging in her satchel.

Maggie pulled on her hat, ready for departure. Suddenly a diary was being spread in front of her.

'Now,' Mrs Thompson said. 'Strike while the iron's hot. How about Friday morning?'

'Sorry?' Maggie glanced at the door, the path to it now clear.

'To come and talk to the class about your work. We'll give you a jolly good school dinner.'

Graham was grinning at her as if he'd set this up. Her mouth dried as she pictured beetroot bleeding into salad cream, her palate clogging with sponge pudding and custard. She had no need to look at a diary; her days were empty white sheets, lacking the old structure of departmental meetings, conferences, or evening classes. She grappled with an impulse to refuse and hurry away; stood her ground a moment sensing Carol's elbow nudging her ribs. Her old self ghosting in a doorway.

'Shall we say eleven o'clock?' Mrs Thompson said, smiling encouragingly, her grey eyes kindly.

Maggie bowed her head to Mrs Thompson's authority,

shrunk back inside her primary-school self, and agreed.

'I'd prefer ten if that's okay,' she said.

At least that way she could avoid staying for lunch.

THREE

A few days later she approached the school entrance. Some attempts had been made to suggest youth and activity with giant plastic butterflies pinned to the brown harled walls and a tiny garden that was now covered in dead weeds.

She'd smartened herself up with a buttoned blouse over her usual old jeans and boots. When Mrs Thompson introduced her again to the class, she saw her own hand trembling against her notes despite the breathing exercises she'd practised on the school doorstep. She used to do this sort of event regularly, but had stopped school visits a while back, only managing to honour commitments to one or two talks for the Women's Institute.

'Primary Five' meant nothing until she'd asked their average age; eight or nine. It was clear that boys likely to cause trouble had been positioned on single tables close to the front. One was slumped forward with his head between outstretched arms. A prod from Mrs Thompson lifted his face, revealing a shock of white flab, eyes half-mooned with dark skin.

'Stays up all night playing on his Game Boy and watching zombie movies, that one,' Mrs Thompson whispered to Maggie in passing. She closed a window against competing noise from a cement mixer working on the school extension.

There were two tables full of girls sitting with straight backs and neatly arranged pens and pencils, smiling attentively in her direction. They were uniform in bright blue sweatshirts but still betrayed self-conscious girliness in the highlighted hair which they preened for each other when they thought Mrs Thompson wasn't looking.

On one of the tables a group of boys swaggered. Their necks were hung with gold chains and their hair shaved into intricate patterns. There was a boy wearing a 'John Deere' boiler suit. All the local farmers wore them in larger sizes. It was like looking at a roomful of miniature adults. They all seemed to have turned up simply to show each other what they looked like – their 'promenade'.

At the back of the room, one table was an exception. There was a collection of girls who were either rather plain-looking or large. They were attentive but unsmiling, like cats disinterested in pleasing anyone. In amongst them was a dark-skinned boy who looked of Indian origin. Callum from next door was there too. And there was another child with a head of long hair, the hint of a small face just visible below a ridiculously long fringe.

Maggie was unsure whether this was a boy or a girl. As she began her introduction the child swept its fringe to one side. One brown, long-lashed eye fixed on her with an unnatural intensity and she heard her speech falter.

She'd brought a PowerPoint presentation and was relieved to take the focus off herself and onto a screen. Standing at the front of the class she felt conscious of her height, almost envying Mrs Thompson's efficient-seeming shortness.

She showed the class some maps of the local area through time

– Roy's military map, Blaeu's atlas; and of course they went back to Pont's early maps and she pointed out how he'd incorporated elevations of significant buildings, shapes of landscape features and writing, including his words about wildness and wolves. She contrasted his style with representational aerial mapping that she was currently doing herself, and showed them educational books to which she had contributed visuals, some of which they knew from their own library.

'What do you think my tools are?' she asked, finally feeling she was into her stride. There was a small show of hands.

'Computer.'

'GPS.'

'Google Earth.'

She gathered in the suggestions, accepting or rejecting, explaining. She was mid-sentence when two words shot out from the long-fringed child at the back.

'Your eyes.' The mouth twisted, suggesting suppressed laughter.

Maggie wanted to respond to the rather unusual contribution. Calculating eyes were exactly what was needed, at least they had been for the map-makers who preceded her. But Mrs Thompson swept things in a new direction.

'Remember not to call out, Primary Five. If you have something to say put your hand up,' she said. 'Now. What questions did we prepare in advance for Maggie? Perhaps we'll take the best one from each table.'

The final question came from the 'misfits' table: 'We're going to draw up our own maps this week. What advice can you give us?'

She swung her legs over the back of her favourite hobby horse.

'Walk.' She heard her voice sparking with a new charge. 'The early mapmakers charted great areas with their own stride, a pencil and paper. It must have made them solitary fellows, don't you think? When I began my career in cartography, people still worked like that. That's where my heart really lies – pens, paper and a feel for geography – not sitting at a computer, eating biscuits and getting fat.'

If she'd had an adult audience, there would have been a murmur of laughter then. Instead there were some fidgeting noises. A couple of the cool boys seemed to be looking at something under the table. The tired boy had resumed his slump. Maggie realised she had lost them and looked apologetically at Mrs Thompson. But then she noticed that at the back of the room, one round brown eye was still firmly pinned to her. She looked back at it. The child stabbed at its fringe with a hand, and the other eye appeared, drawing her in, tipping her attention towards the back of the room. One hand slowly rose into the air, propped on an elbow. She took a breath and opened her mouth.

'Right Primary Five.' Mrs Thompson took charge. 'Hands down please. We'll give Maggie coffee now, and you can have your run around outside a little early. But first, what do we say?'

After the chorus, the scrape of chairs, the exodus, Maggie busied herself, head down, unplugging her laptop.

Mrs Thompson shooed the children out and came to hover near her. 'Super, thank you.'

'I hope I didn't bore them,' Maggie said.

'They've the attention span of midgies.' She obviously thought about this a moment. 'But perhaps not so persistent.'

They had coffee and ginger nuts in the staff room which had a view of the playground so Mrs Thompson could keep a canny eye on behaviour. 'Look at that Sinclair boy, out in his T-shirt in this temperature,' she said.

Maggie noted the girls huddled around a magazine, avoiding boys and football, also visibly shivering in too-thin clothes.

A group of boys including some of the primary fives were playing a team game with a ball. But as Maggie watched, the be-fringed creature walked through the game, intercepted the ball with a subtle flick of the arm and walked on. The child had the slightly loping gait of a boy but the trousers were tucked into pale blue wellies decorated with large white daisies. When its fringe flicked up, she saw the pointed, almost elfin-shaped face, the sudden flash of two over-large, Asiatic-looking eyes, and she was even less sure of the gender. The group of boys didn't protest at the child's possession of the ball. They stood with their hands on their hips for a moment and then turned away and began running at the wall instead, striding up it, seeing who could reach the highest point.

The child took the ball into a corner, balancing and then rolling it: head, shoulder, the sole of a raised foot behind, then back up to the other shoulder. Definitely a boy, she decided. His uncanny dexterity transfixed her, and she laughed out loud. 'Look at that!' she said, but no one in the staff room seemed to share her interest.

Mrs Thompson summoned Maggie's attention back to the room with its steaming urn and a table strewn with educational circulars. 'We're going to have a tiny exhibition for parents in a week or so's time. Just to show them the maps children have been making themselves. Would you come?'

'Of course. Delighted.' It came out with automatic professionalism.

Mrs Thompson smiled and stood up.

Maggie was still wondering about the strange child and the

question lurking unanswered in his raised hand. The round brown eyes. But she stood up herself, seeing that it was time to leave.

FOUR

By the middle of April she was working hard on the atlas for Nigerian schools. Richard had commissioned her to produce the bulk of its pages. Despite a place as illusory to her as Narnia or The Shire, she was starting to draw outlines of the land, filling statistics into pie charts, and translating river systems into diagrams. The main focus was the geography of the West Africa region but it also included reference maps and basic geographical information for the rest of the world, so there was a massive amount of visual data both in map form and statistics that she had to find a way of representing.

She'd superimposed the principal road and rail routes onto a small-scale map of North America, forming a grid of red lines between cities. She noticed that the regularity was surrendered as the main highways approached the 50 degree North line, as if defeated by landscape features or a sparse population well short of the Arctic Circle. It made her feel oddly proud of where she was now, allied to that land mass at the edge of civilisation.

The road networks linking principal cities on the equivalent map for West Africa looked unruly and inconsistent.

'I'm not sure what to do about the population of Lagos,' she said to Richard in one of their phone calls.

'What do you mean?'

'There seems to be no agreement on population figures. Ten million or twenty?'

'Better stick with the UN data, as usual.'

'It's not just that. Shouldn't I try and do a graphic for the pull of the City, why it keeps growing, what that means to infrastructure and so on? It seems so peculiar.'

'Maybe.'

'Any ideas how?'

'I'm sure you'll think of something,' Richard said.

'You're a great inspiration, thanks Boss.'

She sighed when she put the phone down, eased out her shoulders, the muscles stinging from too many hours spent at the computer. Her brain was dull, her eyes heavy despite all the coffee. She looked at her watch, knowing she needed a break, but decided to do another hour before she went out for an evening walk.

She stared on at the map of Lagos. Her thoughts became dangerously unfocussed, scattering to where she would walk, whether she could be bothered to make lasagne later, a vague sense she should phone Carol. Solutions to the Lagos problem dodged her. She stared for too long. It was like sinking into thick water, her hair flapping like slabs of meat over her eyes. The weight of water pressed on her eyelids and yet it seemed she still saw the computer screen, transforming into a cinema of sorts. Shapes gathered in a slow reel. Something red and white appeared; a small figure. An erratic appearance between two parked cars on a roadside. A road she was travelling down. Then there was a close-up; the child's face in profile, her chin lifted, lips parted, bewitched by something on the other side of the road.

Maggie jerked back to her desk, to a lamp illuminating the crisp edges of pages, the grain of paper. She shoved back her chair and put on her boots.

There was no one else on the beach as she was leaving it to return home. Her walks had stretched out with the lengthening days and now she frequently reached the far end of the beach, usually in the evening. An hour or two's walk helped with ideas for work as well as keeping her body from seizing up and rescuing her mind from its shadows.

This time the sea's steady breath next to her had not only pulled her back into the light, but the right map tints for minerals in Sierra Leone had revealed themselves in the mosaic of colours in a rock pool.

The cliffs of Dwarwick Head had been orangey-red in sunlight earlier but now were sullen brown, features blinded by failing light. A couple of black heads out beyond the surf and a car parked in the dunes indicated some surfers, but even the birds were strangely quiet except when a V of geese flew overhead towards the Northwest, the creak of their wings audible. They travelled with such ease and speed Maggie could barely get her binoculars to them in time.

She threaded through a gap in the dunes, crossing the road to a field where ewes guarded new lambs. Voices soared up through the clear air from some council houses marching across the skyline; children doing whatever children do on dry evenings.

When she drifted into the channel of woods which would lead her home it was neither day nor night. The birds had stilled and the ground was dimly illuminated just in front of her feet, demanding sudden interpretation: the rosette burst of a yellowish tussock; bogs that she only discovered when her feet squelched into them. On the lower slopes she snapped against bleached grasses and dead stalks of meadowsweet, luminously pale in the sparse light. When she came to the dark corridor of silhouetted trees higher up, a thick dark carpet of celandine leaves cushioned her footfall.

She knew the way by keeping the gurgle of the burn to her right, the dark rise towards the road and bridge ahead. She came under the arch of some of the largest, oldest trees, gnarled and thick-trunked, with limbs elbowing into the sky. When a noise startled her, she thought of the roe deer she'd seen here before. But this rustle was louder and closer than a deer would come. It carried behind it a murmur, as if from a stifled voice.

A shock of sound above. A shrill cry. She dropped into a crouch. Then something large and dark swung an arc above her. A flutter of air brushed close to her head, and then the thing swung back to her other side. There was a thud in the undergrowth, and then footsteps drumming, tumbling away down towards the burn, an orange buoy left swinging from a rope above her.

She wheeled around, scuffling her hands in dead leaves and moss, clutching at her heart. Leaping up, she strode after the trail of sound which resolved in her mind into children's feet, fading as muffled snorts of laughter grew louder with distance. She stopped at the edge of the bank and peered into a pool of darkness in which one moving thing was just apparent, scampering across a fallen log over the burn and merging with the foliage beyond. She couldn't tell if it was solitary or following others. But she was pretty sure it was human and small.

'Little sods,' she threw half-heartedly after them.

The giggling trail hushed.

She turned back towards the cottage, humiliation simmering in her, and shoved at the orange buoy, sent it back into its now benign arc across the path. She had to duck to avoid it hitting her on its return.

She sometimes imagined a café at the Dunnet end of the beach serving slabs of wholesome cake and huge mugs of tea that you warmed your hands around. In Cornwall there would have been one. But despite the plunge of cliffs, the seals, seabirds and beaches here, Cornwall's characteristic holiday-ness was missing. There were no ice-cream stands, car parks shiny with sun-scorched metal, or clamouring children and dogs. Of course it was out of season but there was more to it than that. She could see that the infrastructure itself was absent. There was just an occasional caravan park or hotel with its signs blown off. Her only port of call was the Sandpiper Centre.

She and Graham stood at the big window, each with a pair of binoculars trained on a sparkling group of white gannets circling on wide black-tipped wings above the waves.

'How was your school visit?' Graham asked.

'Fine,' she said. 'I think.'

'I told you they were rascals.'

'Did you? Well, they were alright in the classroom, but...' The shriek in the woods she'd been trying to shake off since was still trailing her.

'Being cheeky to you on the street, eh?'

'No, not exactly.' She told him then about the snowman intruder who'd welcomed her to the area.

He roared with laughter. When she didn't join in, he said, 'That's kids!'

'They're not mocking me then?'

'Just being bairns.'

So she didn't mention the latest incident. Just kids using the woods as their playground. 'You're right.' She managed a small laugh at her own fears and consciously tried to drop her stiff shoulders, looking out at the horizon; letting it steady her.

The land here barely undulated, lay in stripes and lines in such dark contrast to what was above. The sky was what you looked at. White clouds galloped across wind-driven days; a purple mask formed above the sea at the end of a sunny one; occasional still days cast a milky haze. She looked up more than she ever did in Oxford where there were just snatches of sky between buildings. The anti-windfarm campaigners in Caithness didn't complain about the land being taken away, but about the stealing of 'our skies'.

'Watch yourself now it's gardening time,' Graham said. 'When I first moved up from Stirling, someone kept coming in and deadheading my dandelions when I was out.'

'That's a bit creepy,' she said.

'They didn't want them re-seeding in their own gardens, I suppose. It all stopped when Mary moved in and we started taking the garden a bit more seriously.'

Maggie wondered vaguely if he was telling her this to make clear his marital status. It came as a relief.

'Aye, they've found their breakfast,' Graham said of the gannets, binoculars poised. 'Just deciding whether they want it on toast.'

One of the birds then drew in its wings and arrowed into the sea, returning soon to a surface still frothing with its impact.

'Can dive up to 60 miles per hour, these guys,' Graham said. 'They're wearing crash helmets you know?'

Maggie laughed.

'Little air sacs under the skin of the head and neck that protect them. Eye guards as well. Like racing drivers.' He grabbed his hands onto an imaginary steering wheel and growled the noise of an accelerating engine.

Maggie took the binoculars from her eyes.

'Bang!' Graham said next to her. A gannet cracking onto the surface of water. Knifing through it into a different world.

She felt slightly sick. She was off-kilter, still hearing the imagined car. A terrible skid with a bump at the end of it; a softish sound, not a crack or a bang. Followed by a dragging sensation. She shook her head, shivering it away.

Then Graham was speaking, peering at her, waving. 'Hello?'

'Yes?' she said.

'Lights are on but the house is empty, eh? You're a bit vacant.'

'You what?' She clutched at her stomach.

He laughed and turned back to the gannets.

A knock came on her door on a Saturday morning a week or so later. She was taking the weekend off. A rest from the computer and relief for her creaky limbs. She left her study and saw straight away through the glass there was no one there. Surely not a knock-and-run game this far from the village? When she opened the door to look out she found a parcel lying on the decking outside the door and heard gravel crunch under tyres as the postie pulled away.

A book, 'Home Baking', and a tiny note: 'Hope your first weeks have gone well. Thought this might help pass the evenings now you're away from city lights and missing out on your weekly cinnamon swirls at Joey's. We thought of coming up to see you for the long May weekend, but when John looked it up on the

AA site, he said we'd spend the whole weekend driving. So had to put this in the post instead. Sorry!'

Helen. Still trying to be her friend. Most of them had drifted away from her even before Frank had. 'They didn't drift. You shooed them,' Carol had said. Perhaps what she meant was that Maggie didn't answer their questions. Not unless they were about cakes, singing, or work.

She flicked through the pages. Why on earth would she want to bake? But when she came to photos of plump seeded loaves and salty focaccia with rosemary, her mouth watered slightly and she thought of the loss of her local bakeries and delis in Oxford. Delicious fresh bread was something she missed here where the village shop couldn't do much better than sliced 'Scottish Pride'.

She was queuing for the till in the village shop later that morning with a bottle of wine in one hand, and a bag of 'strong white bread flour' and dried yeast in the other. A refrigerator unit by the door spelled out 'healthy eating' in faded lettering. Its shelves were practically bare, except for some out-of-date macaroni pies and 'Dairylea Dippers'. She tutted inwardly.

'Maggie?'

She turned and looked down on a small, dark woman dressed in what seemed to be jogging gear. Recognition slowly dawned. 'Mrs Thompson.'

'Do call me Audrey.' She smiled. 'How are you?'

'Fine, fine'. She noticed Audrey had children's comics and sweets in her basket.

'I've been meaning to write,' Audrey said. 'To thank you for coming in. The children loved your talk.'

'Oh good.'

'It was helpful for them to hear about it from a professional.'

'Any career plans?'

Audrey laughed. 'That might be going a bit far, though there is one boy. But, well, it's hard to tell with him.'

'Not the one...?'

'With the long hair? Yes.'

'Ah.'

Audrey looked round the shop, and said the name quietly: 'Trothan Gilbertson.'

'It was a bit hard to tell if he was attentive or on another planet,' Maggie said. She imagined the type of parents who would come up with a name like 'Trothan'; hippies probably, into Celtic mysticism. 'Unusual boy,' she said. 'Is he... Does he have...?' Maggie had no idea of the right term for children who had extra help in class.

'Unusual. But he's not been assessed or anything, though no one ever really knows where he's coming from.' Audrey said this quietly, head bent towards Maggie. 'I saw him just now out with his sketch pad, on his own down at the harbour.'

'Doing a map?' Maggie felt a tickle of pleasure at the idea.

'Didn't ask.' Audrey laughed. 'But they've all got their homework'. She nodded her head to show that the queue had moved forward in front of them. 'You haven't forgotten next Wednesday. Nothing formal,' Audrey said. 'We'll make sure you get a cup of tea and a bun.'

'Looking forward to it,' Maggie said, unsure whether she was lying.

Cycling home, she stopped outside the beauty salon housed in a funny kiosk-type building. It was near the boarded-up church, and even as she parked her bike against the salon wall, she could hear the clapping wings of pigeons that rose through the roof of the church and plummeted back in. A massive square front door, big enough to drive a truck into, had been fitted into the front of the building.

She looked at the price card in the window of the salon. There were various therapies available – tanning, pedicures – but also massage, as she'd hoped.

Warm air engulfed her as she went in and some kind of sweet oil hung in it – geranium or orange. There was a small desk partitioned off from the rest of the tiny building, the walls painted a deep yellow.

A woman appeared from behind the partition. She had glossy brunette hair pulled back tightly from her face. Maggie judged her to be about her own age, but well preserved; her skin oily and supple-looking but tango-tanned, her breasts straining against the white tunic.

'Hello,' she said in a London accent, smiling. 'I'm Debbie. Can I help?'

Maggie began to negotiate a massage, wriggling her shoulders as if to illustrate their stiffness.

'It's all your cycling,' Debbie said.

Maggie found this knowledge of her surprising. 'And sitting at a computer,' she muttered.

The massage hurt. About halfway across each shoulder, she felt Debbie's hand play a habit-hardened muscle almost as a string on a musical instrument. She caught it in a lateral movement, pulled it with her and then it twanged back, painfully tight.

Debbie chatted her way through the massage, asking questions. How was Maggie liking the area, what did she do in the evenings and weekends. 'And how did you enjoy your visit to the school?'

'Well, you never know whether anything's sunk in. One or

two might make something of it.'

'I heard you had the class of weirdos?'

'Well. I suppose they were a little ...'

'Couple of right strange kids there. All the way up they've made it difficult for the others.'

'And the teachers I suppose,' Maggie said.

'That Lisa girl? Mother keeps the house full of terrapins. Then the boy who's up all night watching horror movies. I mean what kind of psycho's he going to be? If his dad's anything to go by anyway.'

Debbie appeared to be on a roll, and Maggie let her go with it.

'My hubby Rab – he's a builder – found a lad from that class on one of his sites quite late one night. Got quite a fright. He was hiding like some imp in a corner.'

A strange image drifted into Maggie's mind of a small child nestled in a dark corner surrounded by crusty-shelled terrapins.

'One of the joys of being a builder, I guess,' Debbie steamrollered on.

'Did he do up this building, your husband?'

'He did,' Debbie said. 'It was part of the deal when he bought the church, so we thought we might as well do something with it.'

'What's the church used for now?' Maggie asked.

There was a pause. 'Oh, nothing, really, it's just empty, mostly.'

'Is he intending to convert it?' Maggie heard that her voice was muffled by the towel at her mouth and by drowsiness.

'That would be a big job. It's in a bad state,' and then Debbie picked up her story again. 'Anyway, this lad had picked up something he shouldn't have done, can't remember what it was now. Rab got into quite a ding-dong with the boy's dad when he hauled him home. Told him he had a wild thing for a son. There was nearly a punch-up.' Debbie laughed, taking her hands off Maggie's back she was so rocked by it. 'I've got three. Never had a problem, but then never would've let my kids out at that time of night. And then there's that Paki boy, excuse me but that's what he is...'

Maggie let her go on, nudged the talk away from her so the volume dwindled, the words lost meaning. She focused on the easing of her taut muscles.

Debbie's movements were getting slower, lighter on her back. The towel came up over her, warming Maggie from the neck downwards. She was cocooned. Softened. Pliable.

'Now,' Debbie said quietly, some distance away. 'You'll want to relax there for a few minutes. When you're ready, put your clothes back on and come back through, okay?'

Maggie barely nodded. Her limbs fusing with the couch, she was slipping down; surrendering to sleep.

She was driving. Dusk half-light, and she was driving into the tunnel of trees leading from the village towards the beach. Quite fast. A couple of low branches, like crooked arms, hung down and cracked the roof of the car. She pressed harder on the accelerator. As she passed the Lodge Cottage, a large form dislodged itself from the trees above it, swooped across the road a few yards ahead of her and landed somewhere in the trees on the other side. A huge bird. Before she could do anything, it started to swoop back again. It looked more animal now. Despite braking, the forward motion of the car and the lowest point of the creature's dive met with a harsh crack. It fell into the road, invisible in front of her bonnet. She stamped on the brake, propelling herself into that terrible skid, a sickeningly familiar tide of momentum. There was a scuffing sound and she knew she was dragging something along the road ahead of her, under the bumper; feathers and bone, perhaps fur.

It seemed to take forever to come to a halt.

FIVE

The next morning was warm enough for Maggie to sit outside with her coffee; sun seeping through a milky sky, the wind soft. She found the bare branches of the trees comforting in their way, rather like the sparse lines drawn on the roadmap. The trees were bubbling with birds' twitter today and the rhythmic purr of the sea was just audible. A throaty engine hummed in approach, a boy racer making his way along the road behind the dunes, she supposed.

She looked back to the window-sill where dough stood in a bowl, a small pot belly under a damp tea towel plumpening in the sunshine, supposedly until it doubled in size. The yeast, sugar and warm water had fizzed up quickly, and then she was up to her elbows in fine flour, the dough sticking to her hands annoyingly at first and then becoming smooth and elastic as she worked in more flour. She'd lifted it out of the bowl and pounded it on the worktop. The recipe said to knead for ten minutes so she put on the kitchen timer and didn't stop folding and battering rhythmically with the heels of her hands until the alarm went. By this time her wrists ached, her fingernails were cemented by dough, and she was ready to write back to Helen with an ironic 'thanks!'

But now, as she drank coffee outside, she managed to write something kinder in her reply.

She put on her boots and crossed the field to the woodland, setting aside any irrational jitters. Burrowing down into the little celandine-carpeted glen, she was guided by the burn; a route made her own by her repeated walking. Primroses were suddenly up, bright jewels amongst the green, and the further she went, the louder the sea sounded above the rustle of her feet.

She went first to the old harbour. It had been built to export flagstones and its walls were constructed from a mosaic of its own cargo, erected upright to withstand storms. It had obviously been a peopled place once, an important place which paved the world, but now the harbour water was clogged with seaweed and only a couple of fishing boats remained.

A small figure stood on the pier. As she approached, she could see that the wellies toeing the wall's edge, almost overhanging it, were flowery. She hesitated, thinking she might still retreat, turn back for the open beach where she'd intended to go next anyway, where anonymity was guaranteed. But the head turned, and she saw that the child was holding a pad of paper and a pencil.

She walked to the end of the pier, admiring the stretch of blue ahead of her and the starburst splashes of gannets diving. She turned, expecting to find a face buried in concentration, but although his hand was still poised over the paper, an amused, quizzical look was turned directly on her.

'Lovely day,' she said. A ridiculous thing to say to a child.

'Where's your GPS?'

'I don't really need it here.' She laughed.

'You're not making a map?'

'Not today. It's Sunday.'

'I am.'

The child turned the face of his pad towards her, an invitation which drew her in to look over his shoulder. When she got close to him, she noticed his hair. It was almost damp looking, as if it had dried with salt water in it. She remembered that feeling from her family holidays in Cornwall.

She stepped away slightly but could still see the page. It held a spider's web of fine pencil line. Despite the markings and re-markings, she could see that it was a bird's-eye representation of the Quarrytown end of the bay.

'Gosh,' she said, stepping closer again despite her own resistance. 'Have you done that just by standing here?'

'I went up there too.' He pointed behind them to the small rise of Olrig Hill with its masts.

'Yes', she said. 'You get a great view.' When she went up, she'd seen the butt head of Dunnet lying along the horizon and noticed how even the slight elevation widened the bay into a shiny apron in front of it.

The boy looked up at her. 'Did you hear any pipes?'

'Pipes?'

'Bagpipes.'

'No.'

He went back to his drawing.

'Why?' she asked.

He giggled into his sketchbook. 'There was a man called Peter Barker,' he said. 'He was up there with his cows and met a lady in a green dress.'

'When?' she asked. 'I wasn't wearing a green dress.'

The boy laughed, his fringe tossing out of his squinting eyes. 'He'd fallen asleep for a moment amongst the flowers. She said he could have a Bible or the pipes.'

'Ah, I see. And he chose..?'

'The pipes. He didn't know he could play them, but it turned out he could. His cows did a wee dance when he started to play.'

Maggie smiled. 'A happy ending, then?'

'Except he had to go back and meet her in the same place seven years later.'

'Uh oh.' She sensed the story was about to take a bad turn.

The boy looked up, didn't continue immediately.

'And, did he ever return home?'

'No,' said the boy.

'That's a very sad story then.'

The boy turned his head up to her, one eye piercing the gap in his straggling fringe. 'Why?'

'Well, for his family. His friends. Never to see him again.'

The boy shrugged. 'She was very beautiful.'

She smiled to herself. As if that made his removal from their lives a small thing to accept.

He went on, pointing ahead towards a house that dominated the long flat sward leading out to Dunnet Head. 'And I went up there too.'

'You've been busy.' She wondered if this had all been in response to her talk. Flattering as it might be, it seemed rather an extreme response.

'That was how you said they did it?' he said. 'Taking sightings from the highest places around.'

'Well, yes.'

She looked at his map again and pointed. 'This here, that's the old RAF airfield?'

'Might not be quite right yet. I need to look from Inkstack. Then I'll draw it in properly.'

'With a pen?'

'Aye.'

She grinned at the child. 'Well done.'

He looked back at her as if unsurprised at his own abilities.

'And your mum and dad, have they taken you to all these places to get your data?'

'No.'

'So...?'

No answer came.

She imagined the distances involved for a child of about nine. It seemed a serious endeavour.

'Do you have a bicycle?'

'Sort of.'

'Oh?'

'Well it's my dad's really, but he doesn't often use it.'

She could see he wasn't the sort of child who'd be mucking about jumping puddles on his bike with the other boys, or worrying about where he was going to get designer trainers from.

'You stay in Flotsam Cottage, don't you?' he said suddenly.

She didn't reply. He was a child. There should be boundaries. And that word 'stay' niggled. She knew by now that its sense in Scotland was 'live' but after two months she wasn't sure which she was; tourist or resident. Or which she wanted to be.

'It's here.' He pointed at the cottage on his map, tucked downhill from Sally's bungalow, drawn on his map in partial elevation. Just north-east of it was the sprawl of the derelict farm buildings. He looked up at her, the fringe swept aside to reveal his dark brown eyes. 'Do you think it's right?' the boy asked.

'What?'

'The cottage. Should it be a bit more towards the main road

here?'

'Is it for school, this map? For your project?'

He looked at her as if surprised at the question and then just shrugged. 'I can still move it.' He took out a soft rubber to show her.

'I'll look forward to seeing it when you're finished.'

'I'll bring it round.'

'I meant at the school.' Her voice whipped out quick and hard, a defence; driving him beyond her walls and fences.

She wished she understood kids better. Some, like her sister's, seemed easy to be with and knew their place. She never got anything confusing from them. But then, they mostly ignored her, and she them.

She tried to make up some softer ground. 'Your parents must be proud of you. What do they do for jobs?'

He looked ahead at the sea and the sky before answering. She noticed his profile now, how the forehead almost ran straight into the nose without the normal dip at its bridge, and how the chin jutted out, following the same, single line. It was an odd face, flat and almost ugly as well as beautiful. There seemed something of the Arctic about him; some resemblance to Sami people.

'Dad's a truck driver. He's away sometimes. Mum's in the reception at the doctor's.'

'And you've brothers and sisters?'

'No,' he said. 'I was their only gift.'

Laughter jerked out of her. 'Is that what they call you? Sorry.' It was such an odd way for a child to explain his own existence, and yet there seemed not a touch of irony in it.

He half shrugged.

'You've an unusual name,' she said.

'How do you know?' he asked.

When she failed to answer, he asked: 'What's your name again?'

She hesitated at his directness, but then she had been direct in her questions to him. 'I'm Maggie.'

'The Map Lady,' he said. His eyes were unblinking through his fringe.

She stepped back. 'See you,' she said. 'See you at the school.' Then she turned and walked quickly away, wobbling slightly on the uneven cobbles.

She remembered the dough as she approached the cottage, looking in through the window as she passed. A great dome of tea towel now stood proud of the bowl. She went straight to it, admiring the bubbly appearance of the surface which sprang back into shape when she pressed it with a finger, almost like human flesh. Taking it back into the kitchen, she followed the recipe's next step, 'knocking it back', which dismally reduced its size, and then shaped it to fit two loaf tins which she put back onto the warm windowsill.

She waited, excited by the rapid rise, the sense that something breathing was in the house with her. It reminded her of living with a cat that would shift to a new cushion when you weren't looking or walk without a backward glance towards an open door and disappear for a few days.

And then as the warm dusk approached and the loaves baked, the cottage filled with heavenly scent, insolently redolent of home and contentment.

'You're not going all New Age on us, are you?' Carol asked on the phone that night when Maggie tried to put into words the scent and then the buttery warm texture she'd torn into, slice after slice, still standing next to the cooling rack, not worrying about upsetting her stomach.

Although she welcomed the spring, once May came in Maggie missed the way April's brilliant light had defined everything in skeletal bareness. Her view from the cottage to the sea was obscured now by a canopy of leaves, and when she walked or cycled to the village, the boarded-up church hid behind a thick bank of green so that she almost forgot it was there.

She didn't sleep well now there was more light; her nights became fitful, sweaty, interrupted. And there were her dreams. They'd been infiltrated by the new land. Sea-frayed nylon rope tangled with chips of shell and bone. A stranded puffin carcass washed in with its beak bashed flat and stomach split open to reveal an intricate web of coloured wiring like the innards of an old TV set or radio.

One night she flailed up through the membrane of sleep to find herself gasping and awake. The memory of a wave rolled towards her, over and over, refusing to stop. Each time it arrived on the shore it was ridden by a small red shoe with white polkadots. The sea deposited it onto the sand at her feet. Again. Again. She rubbed at her eyes, swung her legs out of bed, reached for indigestion tablets.

At the window, curtain pulled aside, there was enough light from the moon and the last pinch of day to see by her watch it was just a bit after eleven. Voices seemed to echo out of somewhere nearby, perhaps from the strip of woodland near the cottage, or from the derelict farm buildings, or they were simply carried by the clear air from further afield. They were muffled and remote but then punctuated by loud laughter and shrieks. Youths. She pictured herself storming in amongst them, her middle-aged spinster-self kicking over bottles, sending the culprits scattering. She lay back down for a while with the radio turned up loud.

But sleep didn't return so she got up and made for the beach. She took the usual path through the dunes wondering how long this particular cut through them had been here. They seemed solid and yet under them somewhere was a Church, St Coombs. Graham had told her that the Minister and his wife had to escape out of the manse window during a sandstorm. She wondered how long it would be before the towering monuments shuffled their positions again.

She took off her shoes and slipped down the soft dunes. Grasses, silked by moonlight, prickled her calves. A white sheen of light reflected from the hardened runway of sand. Her arrival on the beach lifted a flock of birds from the shore, only their relative sizes distinguishing oystercatchers from the gulls roosting there. There was a great chorus of peeps, a sense of a single gauzy curtain rising and flurrying in the half light and settling again, further along.

Dwarwick Head soared up to her right and below it the white croft cottages and bungalows of Dunnet village gleamed. To her left the woodland tumbling down to the shore around Quarrytown village was rounded into fairytale shapes by moonlight. She was surprised to see torchlight flickering amongst the harbour walls. Then she heard a vehicle door slamming. Headlights burst the dark open, pointing straight at her. An engine revved and then the lights turned away towards the tunnel-road back to the village.

Two notes launched the rumble of a different engine. She saw a boat move slowly out of the harbour and into the bay. It wasn't until it was well out, pointing towards the horizon that the throttle was opened and the engines whined, fading towards

Thurso.

The quiet and dark resumed, but she felt confused. If she'd seen a light jerking in an Oxford alley, she'd have known it as a student fitting a bicycle light. Here, the map-maker was lost.

A few evenings later, she strolled across the field from the bottom of her lane to reach the neighbouring farm buildings that she hadn't yet explored. She stood in the grass courtyard amidst the low steadings built from local honey-coloured stone. All the slate roofs had caved in and the timbers were sparring up through them. She felt a strange bond with these sad, tipped-up shipwrecks, something similar to watching geese on their angular journeys; a vague feeling of yearning and nostalgia.

She walked through the door of one of the cottages. It obviously hadn't been abandoned for that long. A transistor radio and work tools still lay on a table as if their use might be resumed. The rafters leant against a wall, the tooth ends of them poking up in a row towards the blue sky.

She explored each building in turn, relieved to find no beer cans or bottles, signs of the youthful partying she thought she'd heard. Finally she went into a tall barn that was still partially roofed. Clambering over boards, roofing-felt, timbers and slates, she reached the far corner where a collection of objects made her pause: shells, pebbles and salt-white twists of driftwood. It was as if a tide had run up here, licked this far place, and deposited its sea treasures with a layer of silt and salt. She picked up a curious bit of bone shaped like the fin of a dolphin or porpoise and turned it over in her hands. She couldn't think what creature it could have come from. When she placed it back down she realised that there was a coil of blankets underneath the strange collection. It suggested a small nest, a place where a cat might curl up; a lair, a hide-out. Perhaps even a place for an itinerant to return to, a man with a beard and holes in his boots who'd forgotten how to speak to people.

She looked over her shoulder; an uneasy trespasser in a place she'd thought abandoned. Perhaps she had a neighbour she didn't know about.

Her retreat was only slowed by the threat of rusty nails, but halfway to the door a board lurched and her right foot plunged through it, clutching her leg in its interleaving timbers. She had to drop onto her hands in order to release it and ended up crawling towards the doorway and the safety of the grass courtyard. She hoped no one had been watching. Children were warned against entering unsafe buildings or climbing on their roofs. She'd been foolish.

SIX

The smell of school dinners lurked in the echoey hall. There were small huddles of parents sipping at cups of tea and circulating the tables, each of which was laid out with a group of small sketch maps. They'd been pasted onto sugar paper with the pupil's name below in black type.

'Maggie!' Audrey Thompson was suddenly at her side. 'I'm so pleased you could come. We hadn't heard from you, so we weren't sure.'

Maggie hadn't been sure herself. There had been a pull towards it; something like curiosity, a desire for connection. But a habit of standing apart. In the end the children's maps won; in some far-away corner of herself she wanted to see if she'd made a difference.

'The children will be delighted to show you what they've done.' The small woman grabbed Maggie's elbow and led her to a table where one of the older girls poured her a cup of tea. Maggie noticed Trothan Gilbertson standing with his hair fallen in a great mop over his face, apparently the only exhibitor at his particular table.

When Mrs Thompson clapped her hands everyone in the room miraculously quietened and turned to her.

'Welcome, everyone. We're very happy to present the work of the P5s on their maps.' She went on to introduce Maggie who saw some of the children in the class eyeing her and smiling shyly. She looked into her tea.

Afterwards, left alone, she ambled between the tables, mustering polite comments and encouragement for the children stationed next to each one. In return they were sweet and polite, and she relaxed. Some of them had mapped back gardens, some the main street of the village, but most had stayed within the confines of the school and its playground, which could probably have been done through a window.

Maggie felt herself half repelled from and half propelled towards Trothan's solitary table. It was almost as strong as a prickling on her skin, the strange restlessness she felt when she looked at the boy. It was clear the other children avoided him. They didn't taunt him like they would if he was fat or black-skinned. It was as if his difference to them was so fundamental that he didn't even cross their radar.

Standing beside him was a large bespectacled woman in her late 40s with amber-blonde curly hair. Her chin and neck funnelled into a large breast and she was overweight, but something in her upright posture also suggested a pride in her body. Maggie wondered if this was the boy's grandmother.

Maggie plucked up courage and went over. It was the woman who greeted her rather than Trothan.

At the same time Audrey bustled over. 'Oh good, you've met each other – Nora, Trothan's Mum – Maggie, our friendly cartographer.'

Maggie covered her surprise. Nora seemed like the ageing

descendant of a Viking Princess, and fleetingly Maggie pictured her wearing a bronze bra, horns curving from the sides of her head. They exchanged a few pleasantries, but Maggie had caught sight of Trothan's map and she turned to it while Audrey and Nora chatted on.

His page was scrappy and marked with childish doodles, juice stained, the corners bent and dirtied. But on it was the map she'd seen beginning at the harbour. It still revealed its thin, preliminary lines, the adjustments made by looking at the same portion of land from several different angles. It was sketchy, but he'd taken a much larger area of land than any of the other children, from the harbour right back inland towards Olrig Hill. It included the school, a corner of the beach, and the woody gill leading up to her cottage. The village was there with its neat grids of workers' cottages. He'd drawn in the laundry buildings hovering over the quarry and even marked the site of the Broch down on the coast to the west of the harbour which he'd rebuilt in his imagination into a circular dry-stone construction.

She glanced around the room, curious why everyone wasn't crowding around this particular example.

Trothan shuffled close by and she looked up at him. 'Did you consult the Explorer?'

'Who's the Explorer?'

She took the Ordnance Survey Explorer map from her bag where it always lived and opened it to show the equivalent area. 'Your methods have been very different to the makers of this map, but let's compare them,' she said.

They stood together, looking at the maps side-by-side. The basic land shapes were fairly similar. Trothan had made the sandy part of the beach slightly shorter and narrower than the OS map showed it to be. Significant buildings were pictured as elevations rather than showing their aerial footprint, and hilly ground was revealed in profile rather than through contours.

'I like the fact that your map's pretty accurate,' she said. 'But because of the way you've drawn pictures too, it says a bit more.' She pointed on his map to an area to the south-west of the village where lanes criss-crossed around a stately house; over a bridge; past an ancient burial site.

The child twirled a strand of his long dull hair and looked sheepishly downwards. She remembered his confident stance on the end of the pier. In the school he had the look of a fox in a city slinking along with a low belly, swivelling its head to watch for traffic. His limbs were too long, interests too strange, eyes watchful and curious when he should be detached. He had a sort of unworldliness, and she saw that the best shield for him was his lack of communion and interaction with those around him.

The boy had barely said a word but now he raised a finger over the Explorer map and brought it down decisively. She followed his finger to where it indicated a twist in one of the lanes near Olrig Hill amidst a small knot of woodland. She leant closer. In italicised script were the words, *'St Trothan's Church (remains of).'*

How had she not noticed before? She supposed it was because she was always drawn to the edges of sea and land, hadn't yet explored so much in that direction.

'You've got a saint named after you!' she said, and she smiled into his face as he turned his up towards hers, half hair, half grin. Beyond them, the room clamoured with laughter and footsteps, and the smell of over-cooked cabbage.

A couple of evenings later she regretted being so friendly and encouraging. Walking back towards the cottage, she became aware of something strange about the rail that edged the decking outside. A figure was standing on the top balustrade, a small rucksack bulging on its back. It was Trothan in his flowery wellies. As she watched, he started to skip along it, his arms outstretched like wings, hair flapping at each step. When he reached the corner, he simply skipped around on the spot and continued in the other direction. Absorbed in this promenade, he seemed unaware of her approach.

'Get down,' she said, and saw the balance shocked from him. His knees bent and he pitched forward slightly. Shifting into a jump, he launched himself into the air and came down in a squat in the garden in front of her.

She gazed at him with hands on hips. 'A gymnast as well, then?'

He grinned through the hair which was streaming in a scarf across his face. 'As well as what?'

'An idiot,' she muttered to herself, walking away from him. Then she stopped and turned. 'Where do you live?' she asked.

'Don't you ever drive your car?' he gestured behind.

Cheeky little bastard, she thought. 'Shouldn't you be indoors playing computer games on a lovely night like this?' she asked.

He unzipped his jacket and started to pull something out of it. He looked at her, head on one side, then held out the drawing pad. 'I brought this to show you.'

She hesitated between her wish to get rid of him and her curiosity. 'I saw it on Wednesday.'

He opened the sketch book and almost against her will she was drawn in, so that they stood side by side peering down at it. She could hear his breath, feral and unselfconscious. A smell rose from him, something like leaf mould, saltiness.

It was a fresh version of the same map and he'd added quite a few features since the one she'd seen in the school. 'You're doing it again?'

'This one's better.'

She looked at him. He twisted a lock of hair between his fingers and was sucking it.

'It *is* better,' she said, nodding.

He'd captured the same section of land as the sketch she'd already seen. This time it was more definite and more detailed and it was drawn on a larger piece of paper. The style wasn't contemporary. A suggestion of wolves and sea monsters lurked amongst the lines and shading.

She searched the map for her cottage and found it; a small box next to the big bungalow. It had been perfectly observed, this time as an aerial view.

'How did you do that? Have you got a flying machine I don't know about?'

He sniggered.

'Come on Trothan, tell me. How did you see the shape of the roof as if from above? It's not like there are mountains to climb up.'

He shrugged. 'I just see it in my head.'

A tiny flurry of raindrops sprayed onto the paper. She quickly covered the pad; looked up at the passing cloud.

'You'd better get home then,' she said, handing him back the pad.

He zipped it back into his jacket and waited.

'Where do your parents think you are?' she asked.

He shrugged and then went to the cottage window, and shading it with an arm, looked in. 'Do you work here – making maps?'

'Oy,' she said. 'Yes, I do, but it's also a private house.'

He turned and grinned at her, strangely familiar, and making no effort to move. She had no idea what he wanted.

'Do you draw them like I do?' he indicated his closed jacket.

'You want to see how I work?' she said. 'Is that it?'

He nodded enthusiastically.

Something inside her took a skip. She smiled.

'Do you have a mobile? To keep in touch with your parents?' she asked.

'No.'

His head seemed to hang a little as he shook it. She looked down at him, saw the long eyelashes, a smear of something greenish down one cheek. An ache opened up in her for the lonely child always outside the circle. She pictured him collecting treasured pebbles, imaginary friends, magical stories invented to take place on green hills.

Child. She heard the word spoken as an elderly Irish relative used to say it, spilling in its single syllable the weariness of the adult and their acknowledgment that this slight, bright, hurt-able creature has the same fortune to come.

Trothan looked up coyly, questioningly through his fringe; blinked.

'Well, I would invite you in,' she said. 'But you'll have to check with them it's okay, let them know where you are.' She took out her own mobile phone. 'What's your home number?'

'No one's home just now,' he said.

A latch-key kid. She paused before deciding what to do. At that moment his stomach made a loud growl and they both laughed. 'Want some milk?' she asked.

He looked up at her blankly, not understanding.

She couldn't think what else she had in the house that a child might drink.

'Come in,' she said.

She unlocked the door and let him go in first. He loped confidently across the room in his strange wellies, throwing his rucksack onto a chair, then sat at the long table, back to the wall, surveying the room. It was almost as if he was waiting for something – a meal to be put in front of him or a task to do. She gave him a glass of milk.

'So you want to see how I work?' she said.

He nodded.

'Come through.'

She took him to her Mac in the study and opened up the reference map of West Africa.

'Watch this,' she said. And with clicks of the mouse down the right-hand menu, she peeled away successive layers. She engineered it so that first the text labels disappeared, then the main towns and villages, followed by the railways, roads and boundaries.

'See, all that's left is the shape of the coast, the courses of the rivers and tributaries and the outlines of the islands. That's what mapmakers always start with. We build the rest up in layers. These colours underneath,' she pointed to the land and sea shadings. 'These show relative heights and depths of land and sea.'

He was watching, apparently mesmerised, his breathing audible. 'What's that?' He pointed at a small island, blue-lined, just off the coast of Senegal.

She enlarged it till the island filled the screen. 'Gorèe,' she said.

She dropped the layers back, one on top of the other so that the fort on the island's north end fell into place, the castle at its southern tip, and the label 'House of Slaves' appeared on its eastern bulge.

Trothan pointed at the label. 'What does that mean?'

'It was an important trading post for slaves.'

'Slaves?'

'They rounded up Africans on the mainland, held them in that building till they were taken away on ships by their new owners.'

'Owners?'

'I'm afraid people bought them. They had to work for nothing in places like Jamaica.' She told him then about the Oswalds of Dunnet who must have owned many slaves.

Trothan fell quiet.

She swung her seat around to look at him. 'You could do your own map in layers too. That's how all cartographers work.'

'Have you been there?' he asked.

'No.'

'So how do you know?'

'Just part of my research.'

'Will you show the slaves on the map?'

'Not exactly. This is mostly for a book of geography about now. A reference map. An Atlas.'

His eyes were fixed on the screen as if willing it to represent more.

She stood up. 'Come on, let's look at yours again.'

They went back through to the sitting room table and leant over his sketch pad. 'Have you walked all these burns?' she asked, noting the intricacy of their routes and tributaries.

'Yes.' He seemed surprised that she would doubt it.

'A proper professional,' she said. 'Let's get you set up for doing your own layers. Do you fancy that?'

He nodded.

'You'll have to draw them onto film though. I need the computer myself.'

She dug out several A2 sheets of film and filled her long-unused set of Rotring pens with ink. He settled down at the table with the equipment.

'I'd suggest five layers,' she said. 'Like I've just shown you, except we'll miss out the height and depth shadings. You can start with the shoreline and rivers.'

She could see his project was going to be original and ambitious; that his flamboyant instincts might need some taming. Sensing that she should leave him to it, she stood back a little, anticipating.

He hesitated for a moment with the pen poised over the first film, and then he began to draw.

SEVEN

Trothan came to Flotsam Cottage regularly after that, slipping into a pattern without discussion or agreement. He washed up in the hours after school and always seemed to be starving. She started buying in crisps and baking extra bread. She'd continued to enjoy making bread: the sense of the dough rising, transforming, as she worked on the computer or went out and walked. But she always baked the loaves in the afternoons, so that the homely smell greeted Trothan. She even leafed further into the baking book and found a recipe for butterscotch cake. She remembered having it herself as a kid. He wolfed it as hungrily as she did.

'We never have cakes at home,' he said.

It warmed her afternoon.

Once he appeared with a feather caught in his hair and she often had to resist the impulse to get all his clothes off him and give them a wash and tumble before allowing him to leave. There was too much dignity about the child to treat him like this, she began to realise. But she wondered at the negligence of his parents and whether they knew he was here.

She sent a note back home with him: *'Dear Nora, Trothan has shown a great deal of interest in map-making. I'm happy for him to come and learn bits and pieces from me here after school. I assume you're happy with that, unless I hear otherwise.'* And she wrote at the bottom her phone number.

There was no response.

He used his recent sketches to draw the coastal edges and the burns that led down to it. To this template, he added each subsequent layer. Once he'd got the basic idea, he didn't need that much help. But then onto the fifth layer, which she'd expected to be for text, he plotted the details of the broch remains, World War II bunkers and burial chambers he'd found on his walks. He drew them in confident black lines with the Rotring pen, transferring information from his sketchbooks. A sort of archaeological layer.

In the bay, halfway between the flagstone harbour and Dwarwick Head he drew a cross-shape.

'Is that the Spitfire that went down in the war?' she asked him.

The back of his head assented.

She sometimes worked away in the next room, continuing with her own mapmaking. She'd look through the door and see his bent head and hair fallen forward, the black pen end to his lip as he decided on the position of his next feature. It reminded her of days when she'd worked in the office at a desk near Richard and enjoyed the silent camaraderie of two absorbed brains dealing with space, transferring the world into two dimensions.

But she found herself almost envying Trothan the 'felt' nature of his mapping that drew on evidence from his feet and eyes. All she was doing was using second-hand information; bare statistics. She would never be shoulder to shoulder with other sweaty dancers at Fela Kuti's Shrine, hear the hippos wallowing in Kainji Lake, or weave in a canoe between Makoko's stilted houses in their stinking Lagos lagoon. It struck her that he was more like a geographer, an explorer, to her plain old cartographer.

After each visit, he carefully placed the trace films exactly one above the other, and then rolled them neatly into the cardboard tube that he carried away. She let him take the pens away too, and the set of curved rulers. It was as if he was going to go and do the work somewhere else, but it never seemed that he made progress in-between visits.

The last time she'd seen him he'd been on the sixth, the text layer, conventionally the final one. His annotations included directions like '*the quickest way to get to the cave*'; or place names he'd made up, like '*headland of the shout*' because of a story about a stranded fisherman who'd had to shout to the seals for help; or '*cows' dancing place*'. His long messy scrawls slightly niggled at her own habit of neatness. She considered suggesting a stencil. But then she thought of Pont's maps; his scribbles had been equally undisciplined.

Trothan's next step should be to draw everything onto one sheet of good cartridge paper, ensuring that the features didn't clutter up against each other, that they could breathe.

But then she noticed, but didn't ask why, he cut another sheet of film: a seventh. He reminded her of the story of Peter Barker and the fairy queen.

'Can you put that on a map?' he asked.

'Do you mean the story?'

'Sort of. The place Peter Barker went to. With her. Under the Hill.'

'Well...' Maggie was out of her depth here. Her maps represented what was there, not illusions or hidden places. 'We don't map things like that.'

'Who?' Trothan stared at her.

She shuffled in her seat. 'Map-makers. Not these days anyway.'

'But I can,' he said.

Was it a question or a statement? 'It depends,' she said.

He carried on drawing. The doorway in Olrig Hill materialised.

'It depends,' she continued. 'Whether you want your map to represent what's really there.' He was bent over the page, still drawing, his loose hair brushing it. As she often did, she longed now to tie the hair back, wash it, even cut it all off.

'Maps usually just show real things,' she tried again. 'That's how we usually do it. That's what makes people trust a map.' She was irritated by the self-importance in her own voice.

A brown eye appeared through the hair and gazed at her. 'It is important,' he said. 'Without a door, how could she have taken him down there?'

Maggie laughed. 'Quite.'

But Trothan didn't laugh. He was serious. *Here be dragons,* she thought. And for all she knew, there were.

After he left, she picked up his mug and plate from the table. As she was pushing his chair back under it she noticed marks on the black plastic of the upholstered seat. Two long dull lines remained where his legs had been. She put a finger to one of them and it felt almost as though it were damp.

Graham phoned out of the blue. She'd given him her phone number in case he was leading any walks for the public she might join.

'Haven't seen you in a while,' he said.

She explained that she'd been starting to take her deadline in a month or so's time more seriously. Doing longer hours at her desk had made her body – shoulders, neck, back – feel as creaky as the angle-poise lamp that hovered above her desk.

'Cabin fever, eh? I've just the thing. They're on their eggs,' he announced. 'Thought you might like to come and visit them.'

'Sorry?'

'The sea-cockies'.

'Is this a game?'

'Puffins,' he said. 'We get a few on the Head there. Not the quantity further along the coast, but.'

And so she lay on her stomach on a grassy cliff and watched through binoculars as the black and white clowns entertained with their whirligig flights around a sea-stack. Graham filled her in on scientific facts, but she let most of it wash over her. It was their round-featured comedy that captivated her, and their parrot-looks.

'You just want to take one home,' she said to Graham.

'You're not anthropomorphising by any chance?'

'Yes,' she said. 'I am.'

As the days stretched into late May and Trothan came and went, some of Maggie's childhood memories erupted suddenly, thrillingly, through the strata of burial and loss. Her mother, who was long dead, reappeared raking the garden, wearing brilliant red lipstick as always, with soil smeared on one cheek. Amidst the fruit bushes and neat rows of vegetables, she'd once called Maggie over to look at something in the tilted aluminium bucket, something she had apparently caught in there; a frog perhaps.

Looking over the edge, Maggie had seen the grey sheen of water. But her mother pointed to a rounded, wriggling form catching the light in the shallowest water of the bucket.

'A worm?' she'd asked.

Her mother stayed silent, waited. Not a worm, then. Something strange that stayed tucked against the seam of the bucket's base, but never stopped wrinkling its skin. She had a feeling that any moment her mother might scoop it out and place the jellied thing in her hands, grey and still wriggling. She put her hands behind her back, felt a tight sense of excitement mixed with anxiety in her stomach.

But her mother had instead lifted the bucket so that its base was level with Maggie's eyes, pointed triumphantly to a thin stream of water running to the ground.

'Can you see what it is now?' she asked Maggie. 'It's a leak.'

Maggie was still intimidated by the translucent worm as if it had taken on monstrous proportions.

'But how did the thing make a hole in the bucket?' she finally dared to ask.

Her mother laughed. 'It *is* the leak, silly. The water's making a pattern where it leaves the bucket.'

'It's not a creature at all?'

Her mother shook her head, laughed more. After a moment Maggie laughed too, with relief, and astonishment at the illusion.

Maggie had never been defiant as a child. Her lapses into storm, lightning, sunburst seemed to be associated with being with her more reckless sister. She was too eager to please, or perhaps more precisely, eager not to be in the wrong. She'd been neat and tidy, tried to bring things under control when she was only Trothan's age, tugging ineffectually at weeds in the wildest parts of the garden that her mother didn't reach. She drew precise diagrams in Biology and Geography that harnessed the wild world into two tame dimensions; line and shade. They had been praised.

Now she saw herself as some kind of indulgent aunt to Trothan. The more nonchalance his drawings elicited from others, the harder she encouraged him. When an email newsletter came round with details of a 'Young Cartographer' competition, her cheerleading became more focused. She printed out the form and took it into the school.

Audrey thanked her, but looked at it doubtfully. 'I suppose there might be one or two good enough to send in.'

'I was thinking of Trothan specifically.'

'Oh?'

As if he wasn't obviously special, Maggie thought. 'I've seen his map; I've been helping him.'

Audrey looked up at her over her rimless glasses.

'He's extraordinarily good at it,' Maggie said.

Audrey handed the form back to her. 'Looks like a family rather than a school kind of thing,' she said, pointing to the final line on the form. 'It needs a parent's signature. Talk to Nora; she's the one makes the decisions, I think.'

Maggie looked around her to make sure she wasn't being indiscreet. 'Do you really think she'd be, you know, bothered?'

'Oh they usually are,' Audrey laughed. 'About their wee darlings.'

'Yes, but Nora, she seems a bit...' Maggie struggled, realised she should have thought in advance about how to put this.

Audrey's look now suggested impatience.

Maggie kept trying. 'He's doing more work on the map, the one he did as his school project. But I don't know if Nora even realises.'

'His map. Yes. It's a credit to you that he's taken that up.

We'll put it in the draw for the school showcase in June.' Mrs Thompson now started walking her expertly towards the door. 'One child from each class gives a little talk about a project to all the parents. It gives an idea what's going on right across the school. Why don't you come along?'

And then Maggie was outside, the door clicking shut behind her.

She always tried to be at home at four o'clock which seemed to have become Trothan's regular calling time. One day she was late because she'd taken the bus to Thurso on a mission for speciality flour that couldn't be bought in the village shop. She wanted to try granary, maybe even rye.

She found him sitting on the deck outside the cottage, knees balled up to his chest, forehead touching them.

'Why do you lock your door?' he asked.

'Security.'

He nodded, but looked unconvinced.

'I don't want anyone walking in. I've got computers; they cost a lot.'

'But they could just break a window if they wanted to come in,' he said.

'Don't your parents lock their door?'

He shrugged. 'Not really'.

'Did you talk to your Mum and Dad about the competition?' she asked. On his previous visit she'd told him about it and asked him to discuss it with his parents.

'Dad's away.'

'You showed the form to your Mum?'

Trothan nodded.

'And?'

He shrugged.

'Did she understand that we need her signature?'

'Is there any cake?' he asked.

So. She's not feeding you either, Maggie thought.

If she'd been this child's mother she wouldn't have stood back and let him be ignored and ostracised; working alone, playing alone; tolerated rather than encouraged. Carol had once told Maggie that the first place of a child was supposed to be his mother. If this essential geography isn't established, there can be problems. On the other hand, it seemed sometimes to Maggie that Trothan's primary place could never be another person. It had to be the bay itself, its hills and headlands, buildings and buried things. Perhaps that was just as well.

EIGHT

A text arrived from Carol.

'I'm coming to visit. Arrive Thurso 2035 Friday. Can you collect?'

Maggie was stunned; there had been no discussion of any such visit.

'Why are you coming?' she replied.

'To visit.'

Maggie's work deadline approaching in three weeks tugged at her insides as she went about the preparations – making up a bed in what was established as her study, scrubbing at the toilet she normally wouldn't have to share. Then, after making sure the car would still start after three months' grounding, she gave it a run – a cautious one that had locals revving impatiently behind her – to Thurso for a Tesco's shop. What was on offer at the local shop wouldn't be good enough for Carol. On her return home she sat drinking coffee with a slightly trembling hand and looked around at her refuge. The rhythms marched out by tides, the rising of dough, and Trothan's visits now all seemed slightly threatened. Her sister had been the only one she hadn't been quite able to fence out.

Amidst her fear, however, glimmered a faint excitement: A visitor. She made two loaves.

Maggie saw Carol appear from the far end of the train trailing a small case on wheels. She looked out of place in the cool evening wearing a thin summer dress and flip-flops. Maggie walked towards her, observing her sister's frown, her eyes searching the platform. They were nearly on top of each other before Carol's face livened into recognition.

'Good grief,' she said, holding Maggie at arm's length. 'What happened to your hair?'

Carol continued to stare strangely at her. Maggie felt as if she was in some sort of disguise to her sister: the Medieval Queen or the Lion from their childhood dressing-up chest.

'It was irritating,' Maggie said. 'Around my face. It was too long for my age anyway.'

'You're only forty, for God's sake. It makes your face look so thin.'

'Give us a hug, then,' Maggie said. 'The rest of me's the same.'

Carol drew her in tight then, the familiar smell of perfume or talc about her, the flesh of her bare arms smooth and cool.

'Christ it's cold up here,' she said, pulling away suddenly and turning to walk up the platform.

'I hope you brought walking boots?' Maggie said.

'I came for a holiday, not a boot camp.'

Maggie imagined Carol's bags full of sun cream, shades, trashy beach reading. When they went to Greece together, back in their 20s, Maggie had taken shorts and a T-shirt and stomped off up the hills in rock-cracking heat each day, tutting at the inaccuracy of local maps. Meanwhile Carol languished on the beach and got chatted up by local fishermen.

'I don't often get away without Mike and the kids,' Carol said, as they drove the coast road back to the cottage. Dunnet Head was crisp and proud on the skyline beyond the water of the bay.

'I'm flattered.'

Carol looked around. 'Not much here, is there? Why are there so many abandoned houses?'

Maggie shrugged. 'Not enough people to live in them, I suppose.'

Carol shivered and turned up the car heater.

She gazed around when they arrived at Flotsam Cottage and said, 'You should have reminded me you had so little; I could have brought some of your trinkets up.'

Maggie's paintings, maps, ceramics had been packed up in boxes, a life's memorabilia on hold in Carol's garage.

'I'm enjoying being a minimalist,' she said.

Maggie persuaded Carol into jeans, a fleece and solid shoes the next day, and they did walk a bit. In the evening they picked up fish and chips in the village, stepping their way across a forecourt strewn with prone bicycles in bright oranges and greens. Then they went down to the water's edge and sat on a bench on the grass near the harbour where salmon nets were stretched to dry between tall poles. They looked across the bay to Dunnet Head.

'Funny smell here,' said Carol, sniffing.

After eating, they walked onto the pebbly shore for a while near where flagstones used to be prepared. Maggie noticed a large lumpish form stranded halfway up the beach at the high tide mark. She thought at first it was a live seal, but there was no flicker of movement as she approached.

The skin was black parchment, drum-skin taut against the frame of the skeleton, sagging between the struts and rafters of the bones where the flesh had perished. There was a lifeless zone around it, and the suggestion of a round raw wound on the side of its neck circled by ragged flesh.

'Oh God.' Carol came up behind her. 'How gross. No wonder it's smelly here.'

And then Carol noticed the wound on its neck. 'What would have made that?' she said.

Maggie shrugged.

Carol clutched her stomach and turned away.

'You're not going to be sick are you?' Maggie called after her, but Carol lumbered on, not stopping.

Maggie looked back at the seal. So strong and foul was the smell of rotting flesh, she had to wrap a scarf over her face. The eyes had been pecked out and the skin had started to retreat from the bone of its tail and on its flippers, revealing clusters of thin white parallel bones jointed in knuckles exactly like human hands.

Despite the revulsion, she was attracted to the strange sight of it, almost as if it had been caught in transition between human and seal form. In the water they always seemed curious about humans, swimming parallel with your route along the beach, watching you, as if there was an affinity. 'Fallen angels', she'd heard seals called.

'Why is it dead?' Carol asked when Maggie caught up with her. 'Why did you bring me here to see dead things?'

Maggie thought of all the dead and discarded things she saw regularly washed-up on the beach; a welly without a sole, a guillemot with its head bowed against its chest, a blue fisherman's plastic glove poking its fingers up through the sand as if someone was trying to prise their way out. She loved best the heart-shaped shells of 'sea potatoes'. Porcelain white, they always shattered if she tried to collect them. She'd never seen one when spiny and alive because they stayed burrowed beneath the sand.

She had to acknowledge death didn't hide itself here.

They walked back into a breeze. An old man in a fluorescent jacket had parked his mobility scooter next to the bench and was staring out across the bay. Maggie recognised him. When out cycling the lanes, she'd sometimes overtake him and had been surprised how far from the village the scooter took him. He always had a cigarette in the corner of his mouth, Hell's Angel-style.

He looked up and smiled at them when they got close. It seemed to be an invitation and they sat down on the bench next to him.

'Fine evening, aye, fine evening,' he said.

They both mumbled agreement.

'It's a bad smell, that wee sealie, right enough.'

'It's disgusting,' Carol said.

'I saw you,' he nodded at Maggie. 'Right close to it. Brave lassie, I thought.'

Maggie laughed.

'Do you think it just died of natural causes?' Carol asked.

'Well. You never know,' he said.

'So?' Carol had obviously heard the doubt in his voice, as had Maggie.

'They take an awful lot of the fishies, you know.'

They both waited.

Maggie heard Carol's intake of breath, sensed a speech coming and silenced her with a nudge.

'My son's a fisherman, you know. These are his nets up drying.'

'Can he make a living at it?' Maggie asked.

'On top of his other jobs. I'd prefer it if he stayed on the land myself. Watched him growing up with the sea, of course. But it's a funny thing.'

He trailed off and Maggie wondered what was 'funny'.

'Do you have children?' He looked directly at Maggie.

Died without issue; the words sprang incongruously into her head. 'Carol does,' she said, nodding at her sister.

'Well. It's a funny thing,' the old man continued. 'It's no matter their age, you never stop watching, fearing.'

Maggie looked at his profile. He seemed to bite on his lower lip, his Adam's apple quivering slightly. She noticed some egg yolk stains on the front of his open-necked shirt, revealed inside his fluorescent jacket.

'Especially since she went, you know,' he added softly.

'I'm sorry,' Maggie said. When she looked down she noticed his ankles were bare between shoe and trouser hem.

'Two months now. Still thinking of wee bitty things to tell her when I get home like I've done the last forty years. And then I find she's not there.' He laughed and then drew breath. 'An empty house.'

'Were you a fisherman yourself?' Carol asked.

'A wee bitty. More on the land. But some of these boys, the old boys, they carry around the seabed in their heads, the last valley and rock they know, same as I did with my own fields. They'll take it with them when they go. A loss, that.'

An image came into Maggie's head of the men's bodies lying on the pebbles like the seal's was, their skin blackening, stretching and sagging, all their local knowledge seeping into the water with each rising and falling tide, so it resumed its proper place on the seabed.

'Does your son have that geography in his head?' Maggie

asked. She knew that Carol would have heard the suggestion of the word 'map' and switched off.

The man nodded. 'But you know, there's no one can teach it, nothing at all but time and the sea itself.'

'Like cab drivers in London.'

He looked at her, frowning slightly.

'"The knowledge", they call it.'

'I've heard of that.'

'They're supposed to have larger brains as a result.'

'That right? No wonder these fishermen are so bloody big-headed.' He turned to face her with a broad smile. 'You'll have met them? In the pub?'

'There's a pub?' Carol suddenly re-entered the conversation. 'Shall we have a quick one?'

Maggie had never been to the hotel and didn't find it inviting. Its face onto the street was white, large-windowed, grand almost. But she'd never seen anyone go into its ostentatious front door. The bar was obviously through a door around its side, almost like a lean-to between hotel and laundry, with a semi-permanent row of smokers propping up its outside wall. It wouldn't be anything like Carol had in mind.

'Perhaps another day. I've got a bottle of wine at home anyway.'

They said goodbye to the man.

He looked at Maggie and said, 'Aye well, the sea'll have its way, eh?'

She nodded, confused.

'He was a bit bonkers,' Carol said when they were barely out of earshot. 'Did he mean that the fishermen kill the seals?'

'I don't know.' The image of the round gash in its neck returned. 'But I know someone who will.'

The next day Maggie drove them inland a little way, up onto the plateau behind the beach. There were long straight lanes here, tight and parallel as guitar strings across the peninsula, empty of traffic. Between fields of coarse bog and occasional pasture were dotted a few cottages. Many seemed in a poor state of repair, lashed together with corrugated iron and patched with parts of old caravan. Strange flags flapped alongside them, declaring the eccentricity of their occupants. There was a sense of lawlessness, of people aware that they were living off the edge of the map. Maggie could see Carol's jaw setting.

They passed a woman walking along the road. She wore large green wellies under a full, patterned, almost flouncy skirt, a raincoat over the top. Her grey fringe bubbled out from under a headscarf. Her face spread into a smile when she saw them, revealing a row of gums where her front teeth should have been.

Maggie turned back towards the bay and pulled into the car park of the Sandpiper Centre. She saw Graham straight away, hunched over a cigarette on the dunes. He turned as the car pulled in, and stretched a lanky arm in a wave.

'Friend of yours?' Carol asked.

'That's Graham.'

He ambled over to them, smiling crookedly. 'The car's getting an outing for once, then?'

'My sister wouldn't take a backie,' Maggie said, and then introduced them.

They went into the Centre and browsed the exhibits. Maggie studied the bay through the binoculars and heard behind her Carol quizzing Graham about seals and guns.

'The odd shooting does happen,' he said. 'It's legal around fish-farms and if they get caught in the salmon nets, but it's not supposed to be willy-nilly like. There's been a prosecution of a fisherman.'

'That's terrible,' Carol said.

'Aye, people get right upset about it, probably because they look so much like us.'

Maggie turned to see him opening his eyes wide and then batting his eyelashes. 'Not anthropomorphising, are you?' she said.

'What does a fisherman need who's hard of hearing?' Graham asked.

Carol looked confused.

'Don't answer,' said Maggie.

'A herring aid,' Graham said, and laughed on his own.

'So, stop worrying about the seal,' Maggie said to Carol.

'Plenty selkie stories around here,' Graham said.

'What's a selkie?' Carol asked.

'Seals that come ashore, assume a human form. They might marry, live with a human family and abandon their other life.'

Carol laughed.

'They never go back?' Maggie asked.

'Some stories have the family hiding the skin from them so they can't just make their getaway back to the sea after every stooshie.' Graham grinned. 'Bit like how I hide the car keys from the missus now and then, I suppose.'

'I thought this was a scientific centre,' Carol said.

'I guess it's a metaphor,' Maggie said.

'A metaphor?' said Carol.

'People who feel pulled between two worlds, who're not sure they fit in.'

Carol pulled a face.

Maggie persuaded her down onto the big beach, hoping

Carol would enjoy it as she did. Nothing stayed the same between the tides here. A chain of footprints in the sand would be patterned by tide-drift into blurred tweed. Grasses tumbled by the waves got matted into shapes resembling a cat or a whale, or were formed into curiously solid balls. Tree roots took on the pale satin patina of bone, washed up after being picked clean by the sea. She was always doing a double-take. Thinking she'd seen something from the corner of her eye - a figure or a bird – and then making it vanish by turning her gaze on it directly.

She wondered after his selkie stories if Graham appreciated the mysterious as well as the scientific. It was after all through him that she'd learnt about birds flying underwater, dunes shifting silently in the night to consume a church. One thing became another. Timber to bone. Shell to sand. Sky in a transfer with sea.

Being with Carol returned her to a different perspective. She thought of the solid streets of Oxford, great canyons of rock that she'd cycled through. Edifices that were dependable and unchanging.

They walked towards Quarrytown. The weather had got cooler and gustier again and the day snatched at her, quick and bright as the clouds sprang apart, racing through her blood faster than caffeine or wine.

She tugged at Carol's arm. 'Come on.'

'What?'

'Doesn't it make you want to run?'

'Feel free.' Carol plodded on, hunched against the wind with her hands deep in her pockets.

Maggie spun away from her, arms outstretched. She was airborne and flying, or at least spinning and spinning on the wet sand, and then swooping back, breathless, to Carol's side.

'What's got into you?' Carol asked as Maggie linked arms with her. But Maggie could tell from her half-smile that Carol was glad to see her like this. 'You always could be a wild child,' Carol said, indulgence in her voice and that implied, 'before'.

Maggie let go of Carol, her arms falling to her sides, dropping back down into steadiness, head bent. A flightless bird.

Not long afterwards Carol said, 'We've walked far enough now, haven't we?'

They turned back, watching at a distance as a small family group gathered around a young girl cradling something in her coat. The family peered in at whatever it was, and then the group looked towards the dunes and set off towards the Centre, the girl walking fast at the front, her upper body pitched slightly forwards.

'Must have found an injured bird,' Maggie said.

When they got back to the cottage, Trothan was sitting at the table hunched over his map with a pen.

He looked up when the door opened and Maggie smiled when she saw the full brown eye peeking up through the fringe. Trothan knew she'd stopped locking the cottage door, but he'd never just come in like that before.

Carol jolted visibly when she saw him.

Maggie went over, unable to resist looking at his latest creation. 'Carol, this is Trothan, my mapmaking colleague.'

Carol nodded slightly.

'Come and see,' she said, but Carol ignored her, carried on taking off her coat.

Maggie noticed that Trothan was working on the seventh sheet of film again; the layer that seemed to be for his stories.

He was drawing features onto the big scoop of the bay, into

the large area that was, as far as she was concerned, empty; the water itself. She decided not to go into why this wasn't a great idea, why the text usually tops everything; to leave it until Carol wasn't there.

She caught sight of something drawn into the bay at the north-west, beyond Dwarwick Head. She laughed. 'What's the story here?' She didn't want to break Trothan's concentration, but she did want to know why, near a drawing of a mermaid, a cave had been suggested in the Cliff and within it a pile of coins and a man with a chain around his ankle.

Trothan raised the pen and put the cap on it. 'This man,' he pointed at the shackled figure. 'He said he loved the mermaid. But really he just wanted her treasure. So she took him down to her cave and kept him prisoner.'

Maggie looked up smiling at Carol, but she was stone-faced, averting her eyes.

'And is he still there?' Maggie asked, smiling.

Trothan nodded and stood up. Just before he began rolling his layers of film up, she caught sight of two drawings on Olrig Hill. A bagpiper was being led into a door in the hillside by a woman. She knew that one. But a small stone hut was also marked on the north side of the hill.

'What's that?' she pointed at the hut.

'That's where they did the weaving,' he said.

'Who?'

'The women. Twelve women.'

'Right. So it was a woollen mill. Did they make blankets?'

Trothan shrieked with laughter.

'Tweed then?'

There was relish in his voice when he said, 'They wove with men's intestines.'

She saw then that there was also a strange structure hung with human skulls. A flock of large black birds were scattering from it. 'That's nice.'

'And the loom was weighted down with human heads,' he said. 'And the thing that went across...?'

'The shuttle?' she suggested.

'The shuttle was an arrow. Or maybe a sword,' he said.

'Who were these women?'

'They told who would die in battle. It's like a prediction. And when they'd finished they attached their horses to the cloth and galloped away. Six went north and six went south.' He linked his fingers together then tore them apart, making a sucking sound for the tearing of the intestines. Then he looked up at her from the corner of his eye to gauge her reaction.

'That's a gory story,' she said, flickering a glance to Carol, who was looking away.

'It's not a story.'

'Oh?'

'There was someone who saw it. A man called Dorrad.'

'And how do you know this "not-story"?' she asked.

'My dad told me.'

If she could create a beast from a tiny turbulence of water in a bucket, why shouldn't Trothan imagine such things? He harnessed a chaotic world into line and shade, just as she herself did, but now he was including the occult, hidden things in the land. If Carol hadn't been there, she'd surely have hugged him for his ingenuity, forgiving his diversion from mapping conventions. She might even enjoy a little pride in the sense that she'd helped initiate this originality. She just grinned and gave him a tiny pat on the shoulder as he turned away from her.

He was heading for the door, passing Carol. She saw him turn briefly, raise a hand in goodbye, saw that his face was serious and noticed again its strangely flat profile. Then he was out of the door, skipping past the window, hair flying behind him above the little rucksack. She felt a whisper of worry that he might be upset or offended.

Carol hadn't moved.

'So,' Maggie said. 'Glass of wine?'

'Who the hell was that?'

'I told you. Trothan.'

'What was he doing here?'

Maggie was heading for the kitchen. 'Chardonnay or Rioja?'

'Maggie, what was that creature doing here?'

Maggie walked back in with two glasses. 'He's a gifted child with an interest in maps.'

'He comes round here? Lets himself in?'

'Seems to.'

'Do his parents know?'

'Yes.' Maggie put the glasses down and held the bottle of white wine up to show Carol, questioning with a cock of her head. She poured out a glass and handed it to her.

Carol prowled the room, frowning slightly. Maggie took a seat on the sofa, put some music on. 'Want some nibbles? I've got pistachios.'

'Maggie,' Carol said carefully, sitting down. 'What are you doing with a strange hippy child wandering in and out of your house?'

Maggie laughed. 'He's not a hippy.'

'And why did he take off like that when we came back?'

'Because of you probably.'

'Me?'

'He's a sensitive boy. Runs off if things crowd him. He

probably picked up on your hostility.' Anyone would have, she thought.

'Maggie, I'm serious. What's he to do with you?'

'You should have looked at his map.'

'What about that gross story?'

'All boys like stories like that, don't they?' Despite herself, Maggie shivered slightly at the thought of the intestines. 'I'm just encouraging his talents.'

'He goes to school, doesn't he?'

'Of course.'

'He has parents?'

'Seems to.'

'So why have you adopted him?'

'I've not adopted him. We just have a professional interest in common.'

Carol burst out laughing. 'He's a child.'

'Obviously.'

'Children get into all sorts of things. They live in the moment. They don't have projects or professional interests. Bloody peculiar child if you ask me, to be so driven.' The nursery nurse lecturer at her work.

There was a pause in the discussion while they drank some wine. Maggie would have liked to start a new topic of conversation, but although Carol's demeanour was gentler and her voice softer when she looked up, she was still on the same tack.

'Maggie,' she fiddled with her glass. 'Is it that you think he can heal something?'

This new idiocy shot Maggie to her feet, making her slop wine onto the floor. She stood up and strode out of the room to get a cloth from the kitchen.

NINE

The next day they went to John O'Groats, visited tat shops, as if in pretence that they were in the cream-tea comfort of Land's End. They had to wrap up in several layers and ate their ice creams in the car to keep it free from their wind-lashed hair. The simple pleasure of sitting on a wall in balmy sunshine and watching other tourists wasn't going to be replicable here.

A few bedraggled, wind-scorched cyclists and walkers doing the 'end-to-end' arrived or departed, were greeted with hugs and champagne, but soon retreated to shelter.

'If this is summer, I'd hate to be here in winter,' Carol said.

'It's not always like this.'

'And will you be?'

'What?'

'Here in winter.'

'I live here.' The realisation arrived in the moment of saying it; a sense that she *could* stay, that the place might allow her longer than six months.

A couple of sunny days followed. They visited Peadie Sands, walking over Dwarwick Head from Dunnet to reach the small white-sanded cove where the sea was turquoise and geology laid bare. The mermaid on Trothan's map had disturbed Maggie's idea of the place. Now she felt she might put her bag down on a rock and find it displaced to another one. The waves here might sing a story.

'People swim here,' Maggie said.

'Swim!' Carol looked horrified.

'Not me.' She hadn't swum for years, and even then it had been in a warm swimming pool with her neck erect and hair dry. The North Sea was hardly a temptation. They walked on.

Maggie found it hard to enjoy the place with the sense that Carol was so at odds with it. She seemed to be happiest indoors in front of the TV when she was absorbed into programmes that were equally familiar at home.

'It's like being abroad,' she said once, and looked out of the window. 'Without the heat.'

Maggie didn't want to show Carol that anything had changed since their conversation, but as they tended to be out at the times Trothan would normally visit, she locked the door after them. Perhaps the boy shouldn't be coming in and making himself at home. She missed the ritual of his visits on those days. She almost wished Carol away so she could open the door up and have him back instead.

As much as anything she missed seeing his map materialise. It was a mysterious process; she just watched and tried not to interfere, as if she might somehow put off his 'sight'. She half expected the prehistoric fish that had swum between the strata of rock here to appear as scaly decorations along the shore on his map. Or perhaps the shadow caused by a large flock of birds, known as an 'angel' by radar controllers, would appear sweeping a course around Dunnet Head. She hoped he was still working on it, wherever he was; that he *could* work at home.

Having Carol there forced her to get used to driving again. Perhaps that was part of her intention. Frank's tactics to get her back behind a wheel had been gentle, but transparent. He'd circled second-hand cars in the small ads of the local newspaper and left them lying on the kitchen table. She put them straight in the recycling bin. She noticed, but looked away, when frustration curled his shoulders.

Back then he'd helped keep her in suspended animation; the exchange of news at the end of a work day, someone to go to a film with or walk with at weekends. Other people helped with that too. There was still night and day; eating and sleeping; work and play. She learnt to do what was necessary, the bare essentials that kept those around her from saying, 'it's not like you,' or advising, 'you need to...' or worst of all, asking how she felt. She acted out the numb normality of wine-sipping in front of the TV on a Friday night, the phone calls to Carol and occasional evenings with friends. No one knew about her dreams or the images that insisted themselves onto a blank computer screen. They didn't see the red shoes, the white polkadots. She kept everyone at bay.

'Time,' they'd all said, even though she hadn't asked them.

Eventually Frank gave up circling cars for her. Presumably he'd circled a job advert for himself instead. After a year he put his head in his hands and told her he'd taken a new job in another city. And he'd rented a flat on his own.

'I feel terrible,' he said, his mouth twitching in an odd way at one corner.

Maggie had nodded, accepted, forgiven. How could she blame him?

After Frank left, Carol phoned with a new regularity. Most

weekends Maggie would make the trip to stay with Carol's family, eat shreddies with Fran and Jamie on Sunday mornings before the orchestration of family life swallowed the day with lifts to parties, football, pony-riding. She usually took the train there. Once or twice she caused consternation by arriving on her bicycle.

'Stop punishing yourself,' Carol had said. 'It wasn't your fault.'

Carol wasn't the only one to say it. Her GP had said something similar when she went in for 'something to help her sleep'. Friends said it too. The police pressed no charges. Even the formal inquest seemed to absolve her in less personal terms. And it came in the silence of the girl's family.

Then Carol had calmly told her that the girl's parents had split up. It was what happened, Carol said, with all the stress. And Maggie had started the small ads search herself, for a new house and a car.

'Don't you want a bit more company?' Carol asked her on their penultimate evening.

'I'm a company of one.' Maggie looked up at her. 'You have your husband and children to anchor you.'

'When the children are young, they expect me to be an anchor, of course they do.'

'But they anchor you too. It doesn't matter where you are,' Maggie said.

'What do you mean?'

'Your location is your family unit. I've got this place instead. The beach. The bay.' Maggie gestured out of the window.

'But what about a normal life?'

'This is normal life. I can work here as well as anywhere.

I've got food and washing facilities. I've not gone to join a cult, starve myself to death, if that's what you think. I've always loved the sea.'

'Yes, at Exmouth or Budleigh Salterton.'

'I can buy Devon clotted cream in Tesco's if I want it.'

'And what about friends?'

'I haven't seen them in Tesco's, no.'

'Ha ha. Do you have any?'

'I've only been here three months,' Maggie said. 'And I know Graham. He's alright. He likes birds and he likes bad jokes. Which is fine with me.'

'But you've not even tried to join a club, you don't go to the pub, restaurants. Why are you being so odd?'

'Odd?'

'Yes.'

Maggie's face flushed. 'Come on now, haven't I always been "odd".'

Carol went quiet then. Maggie had never had a carefree attitude as a child like Carol had. Her mother was always reassuring her, 'It's all right. You're not in any trouble.' Meanwhile Carol had seemed to breeze on through life.

Maggie felt a need to lighten things. 'You're just afraid I'm going to turn into that woman we saw yesterday,' she said, imitating the gummy smile.

'Yeah, or one of the weirdos living in the falling-down houses,' Carol said. 'And what about love?'

Maggie saw that her diversion had failed. 'Love?'

'Yes, finding love. You haven't given up on it, have you?'

'Carol. My head is bursting.'

'I mean there was that nice chap you worked with. Didn't you want to pursue that?'

Maggie thought hard. 'Richard? You mean Richard? He's my boss now, for God's sake.'

'So?'

'He's 600 miles away'

'No,' Carol said. 'You are.'

Maggie gave in and they went to the pub on Carol's last night.

'I can't believe you've not been to your local before,' Carol said as they reached the door.

'I'd rather spend my evenings out in this light.' The sky gleamed over and around them, swirling with birds.

The door slammed shut, temporarily blinding them as if in illustration of Maggie's point, and they fumbled down a corridor towards another door. It gave onto a small bar with formica tables and woodchip walls, a fruit machine and a pool table. A couple of men sat at the bar; one bald and bulky, the other dark-haired and wearing a check shirt. Otherwise it was empty and there was no one serving.

The two men looked over their shoulders as the door opened, muttered greetings, and then turned back to each other. Carol took the initiative, stalking to the bar and pronouncing in her south-eastern vowels, 'What do you have to do to get a drink here?'

The men indicated a bell.

'I'm having a G and T,' said Carol.

'Okay. Me too.'

The bartender, a young man with a ponytail and a sniff, eventually came and delivered the drinks. They settled themselves at one of the tables on red velvet stools.

'Thanks for my holiday.' Carol held up the glass.

'Come again,' said Maggie.

The door opened and more people came in. Two young lads who looked barely 18, and an older man with a dog and a stick. A gradual filling and warming of the bar. All of them greeted the original two men, nodded vaguely at Carol and Maggie. When Maggie went to the bar for refills, the bald man turned and half smiled. 'On holiday?'

'My sister is.'

'And you?'

'I live here.'

'Oh.' He looked surprised, questioning. 'Been here long?'

She explained, and when he asked if she liked the area, she clearly gave the right answer. The slight whine and chittering rhythm to his speech marked him as a local. When he asked where she stayed she was vague, fluttering her hand in the general direction. 'A cottage, up that way, a bit out of the village.'

'You're not the Map Lady, are you?'

'I'm a cartographer, yes.' She smiled.

'We've heard of you of course, from the weans.'

Despite herself, a breeze of pleasure tickled her. 'What about yourselves, what do you do?' she asked.

'Dounreay, me,' said the check-shirted man. 'Till they finish decommissioning or I retire.'

'And I've the butchers,' the bald man said. 'Not seen you in yet.' He picked up one of her slim wrists, inspected it, laid it down again. 'Not vegetarian are you?'

She laughed. 'Not deliberately.'

'We're just across from the chippy, any day except Sunday. We'll feed you up a bitty.' He said it as if he could smell steaks sizzling.

'Does anyone sell fish locally?' she asked.

The men shifted on their seats, exchanged glances.

'There's Tesco's,' Archie said.

'I've this romantic notion of going down to the harbour and buying it straight from the fishermen. I suppose it doesn't work like that.'

She laughed at herself, but the two men stared back, smiling glassily.

'Let's ask Jim.'

She realised they were looking over her shoulder at a younger man with a weaselly face standing at the bar in yellow wellies. He nodded at her, ordered his beer, and remained there. He had a sidekick – a scruffy-looking man wearing a cloth cap that he didn't take off. His otherwise rather boyish face looked leathery, as if you might find it stitched and scuffed like a saddle. He was perched on a bar stool, knees wide apart, sou'westers pulled down around his waist, advertising that he'd come straight off a boat.

'Lady'd like a wee fishy, Jim,' the Butcher called over to Yellow Wellies. 'Can you help?'

'Aye,' he nodded into his beer.

'You'll oblige, eh?'

He raised his eyes then. 'Flotsam Cottage, is it?' Crooked eyes on her, a slight grin.

'Yes,' she said uneasily.

'We'll bring 'em up.'

'That's how it works?' Maggie asked.

The grin widened and the shoulders of the sou'wester man next to him shook in silent laughter. He wiped the back of his hand across his mouth. Maggie wasn't sure if she was the butt of the joke or if she could share it.

'Ach, they might be a pair of villains,' the Butcher said. 'But you can at least trust them with the fishies. Fresh out the bay.'

She smiled despite feeling out of her depth and quite possibly a little tipsy from her G and T. When she took the drinks over, Carol said quietly, 'So do you think that's his son?'

'Who?' Maggie asked.

'The man in the wellies. Son of the bonkers scooter man?'

'No idea,' said Maggie.

Carol phoned her family as usual that night and Maggie could hear the excitement in her voice.

'I'll see you tomorrow night. Well, you'll be in bed fast asleep, but I'll see you, come and give you a kiss. The train takes forever.'

Afterwards, Carol turned the conversation towards what Maggie had left behind. Maggie's palms sweated.

'How's that nice old lady managing without you?' Carol asked. 'You know, the one next door you used to take chocolate and gin into?'

Maggie laughed. 'Mrs Henderson.'

For some time Mrs Henderson had been part of Maggie's routine. She'd pop in at least once a week and they'd sit and drink dark brown tea together while Maggie listened to stories of her glory days in the WRENS. She remembered once laughing so hard that she spilt tea over the white linen cover on the arm of the chair. But it hadn't seemed to matter. The story was more important.

'You got her into all sorts of trouble with her family, didn't you?'

'They didn't approve of the gin, apparently,' Maggie said. 'But Mrs H did.'

'How will she get her fix now?'

'I don't know.' Maggie didn't want to admit that her visits had fizzled out, grown infrequent, in direct relation to the way the old lady had looked at her, the blue eyes suggesting she was about to ask questions. The memory scorched now. 'She's got much better-qualified people to help than me, I'm sure,' she said.

'You only need to be human, don't you?'

'Quite,' Maggie said, and stood up. 'Cup of tea?'

She went to the kitchen and chewed through four indigestion tablets as she waited for the kettle to boil. She wondered how she was going to feel after Carol left, whether the guilt-hounds would follow in her wake, hunting Maggie over the flat wet plains.

TEN

Trothan and Maggie were both working at the sitting-room table when a vehicle pulled into the drive. She stood up and looked through a window, saw a van with 'Rental Refrigerated Transport' written down its side, and weasel-faced Jim of the yellow wellies approaching with a plastic tray.

She opened the door.

'Fish.' Jim's eyes flicked up onto her. 'You wanted some, eh?'

'Sure. What've you got?'

He pointed into the open box. 'Cod. Haddock. Coley.'

'It'll freeze okay, will it?' she asked.

Jim looked up to answer her and his gaze jumped over her shoulder. 'Hi-aye, wee mannie,' he said.

Maggie looked around. Trothan was standing barely two paces behind her, still and silent. His wide-eyed stare was trained on Jim. He made no answer to Jim's greeting.

'Trothan?' She prompted politeness as she imagined a mother would, but he remained there, unblinking. She turned back to Jim. 'Two of each, please,' she said.

After she'd shut the door on Jim, Trothan followed her to the kitchen, watched her stow the fish in the freezer compartment.

She went back to the table and the child lurked in the doorway, looking unhappy. He'd been playing on her laptop with some of her map-making software and using Google Earth to look at the local area. She noticed he'd magnified the old boarded-up church. It sat obliquely to its surrounding square of woodland, contained and monumental.

What's in the old church?' she asked him. It was a missing tile in the mosaic of her local mental map, and therefore an irritant. 'Trothan?'

'Yes.'

'What's in that old church?'

'Nothing.' He sat back down at the laptop.

'Have you been in?'

He nodded, started making tiny flourishes with his mouse hand, corresponding to flickers of his fringe.

'Well come on, what's it like?'

'Just space.'

'Is there any furniture? Pews?'

'Nothing.'

'How many floors?'

'None.'

'None? You mean you can look right up into the roof?'

He nodded. 'There's a gallery thing. High up around the edges.'

She stood up, pushed away his hand and closed the lid of the laptop. 'Come on.'

He looked at her.

'Let's go and see. You obviously know how to get in.'

'Okay,' he agreed easily, stood up. 'We can go through the woods.'

'Can we?'

'It's a shortcut.'

At least he looked happier now.

Once into the trees out of the bright afternoon light, he led the way, jigging down a steep, mossy bank towards the burn. She paused. He stood below her by the side of the burn, elfin-small amidst a tangle of green foliage and the gurgle of water.

'Come down on your bum,' he grinned up at her. 'It's easier.'

She sat down on the moss and used her feet to ease herself down, laughter jerking out of her as she slipped, gathered speed, lost control. She felt her knickers getting damp through the back of her jeans. This and the foxy smell of the earth and tree-mould brought back a memory of the soily bank in the garden that as kids she and Carol had slipped down, whooping, for hours one afternoon, till their backsides were black and they'd worn shiny runnels in the earth. It turned out that their father had recently re-seeded the bank and his scolding had sent her shrinking away to a sour corner to deal alone with her burden of wrong-doing. Meanwhile Carol just started a new game.

'You're just trying to humiliate an old woman,' she said to Trothan when she struggled to her feet at the bottom. Her hands sank into the peaty soil and came up blackened and stinking. She waved them, clawlike, in his face.

'Which way?' She looked around. There was no obvious route from here. The burn was ahead of them overlain with a mossy lattice of fallen trunks, which Trothan now pointed at.

'This is the way I always come. It's easy.' As he said it he was jumping on and off a small trunk.

She shook her head. 'For me?'

'First you step onto this trunk,' he skipped onto it. 'Then you have to do a wee wriggle to get around this poking-out branch.'

And he was around it and in two straight steps on the trunk the other side.

'For goodness' sake, Trothan.'

He was standing on the far bank, hands by his sides, face partially covered by his fringe. But when she said this, he scurried back across and stood on the trunk, hands out.

She put her right hand in his as he stepped expertly backwards, guiding and steadying her as if his route here was instinctively programmed. She moved forward two steps and now grasped the branch that she was supposed to wriggle around. She looked down. The burn was three feet below her, flowing fiercely and rocky-bottomed.

'Lean out. Put your weight on it,' he said.

'Lean out? You're kidding!' But she finally took his guidance and swung her body out around the protruding branch. Then she moved forward a few easy steps. By the time she reached the far side, she was laughing again.

He led her next up a flight of crumbling steps mossed into the far bank, and then up onto even ground, crossing a field and skirting the council houses to a broken barbed-wire fence which they stepped over. It brought them into the churchyard.

The grass was long and hazards poked up from just under the surface; car sumps, headlights, bits of seat. 'God's workshop,' she thought. Trothan led them to the large door in the stone wall of the church, festooned with heavy padlocks. At the bottom of this was a hole the size of a cat flap.

Eventually she looked at Trothan. 'So? Where do we get in?' She was curious to see inside now.

He pointed at the small hole.

'There must be an easier way – perhaps through one of the windows?' She was ten years old again, determined to press on with an adventure.

'Someone boarded them all up,' he said.

She looked at the hole. 'I can't get through that.'

He shrugged, and then was on hands and knees, twisting and wriggling until just his wellies writhed on the grass, and were finally drawn in. She chuckled at the sight of him apparently being 'eaten' by the church.

'I can't, Trothan. You're on your own in there.'

There was a sudden, loud clapping above her head. She looked up to see a hand of pigeons burst out of a vent in the roof and clatter away into the trees. She stopped laughing, and put her ear to the wooden door. Trothan's feet were making an earth floor reverberate slightly as he walked. And then they stopped. She got on her hands and knees in the damp grass, put her head to the hole and tried to look in. She could see a car seat and a couple of boxes, but it was too dark and she couldn't twist around enough to look up.

'Trothan?' She called weakly through the hole, hearing the syllables echo inside, unanswered. She thought she heard some scuffles coming from higher up. She called again, louder. 'What are you doing?'

She pulled herself back from the hole. A sudden shower began soaking her jumper and she was cold.

She put her head to the hole again and called in. 'Trothan. It's raining. I'm going back.'

No answer.

What had she done? Perhaps he'd found some ancient tunnel used by smugglers in darker days and was now crawling along it towards the harbour. She imagined the headline in the *John O'Groats Journal*: 'Parents in vigil as boy buried in mystery tunnel', and her name connected with the tragedy. The weight of responsibility gnawed at her. It was so sudden, this transition from childish adventure to adult concern. She didn't even know where his parents lived, should she need to go and confess.

She heard creaking coming from higher up in the building. Her face felt cold. She bellowed his name again.

She moved around the outside wall. Hanging from some brambles she found a collar. The name 'Tara' hung from it on an engraved disc. A disappeared cat.

Picking up a plank of wood, she rested it between the ground and one of the windows that was still glazed and not boarded up, and then tried to crawl up it. But halfway up she lost her nerve. It was too high. She was soaked now, her hair dripping.

Hands on hips, gazing up at the window strung with cobwebs, its surface occluded, she thought she saw a pale face staring from behind it, swaying slightly from side to side and then pirouetting. It was as if seen through fathoms of green water; a drowned sailor with huge pitted eyes floating just beyond the window. Then suddenly with a flick it was gone.

'Trothan!'

The face had been a good ten feet off the ground. What the hell was he doing?

Her knees trembled and she felt her groin tightening. She stumbled back round to the wooden door and kicked at the small hole. The timber gave slightly, and she knelt down and wrenched at it with her hands, enlarging it enough to get her head through up to her shoulders.

Finally her eyes adjusted and she could see up to the wooden catwalk that clung precariously to three inner faces of the walls. An inverse vertigo swayed her. It was as if she was looking up into a vast guano-reeking cavern. She called his name again, but her voice just dislodged pigeons who left a trail of pneumatic trills as they lifted to the roof and then clattered through the fanlight. Then something large swung across her vision attached to the end of a rope, hair flying out behind it, ten or fifteen feet up. Trothan. The rope tick-tocked backwards and forwards, slowing, and when the pendulum finally centred, he let go and plummeted into a pile of something at the back of the building. There was a soft scuffling noise, a pause.

'Are you alright?' she called.

And then she saw his flowery wellies running back towards her, towards the hole in the door.

She withdrew while he wriggled out. Concern turned to anger now. 'This is a very dangerous building. You do realise that? Do your parents know you come here? A featherweight would rip that catwalk down – you weren't up there, were you?'

He was impassive. It occurred to her in the hiatus that followed that it had been her idea, she had incited him to do it. The adventure of getting here had been his, that was all.

'And I'm soaked, look at me!'

She noticed that his hair and clothes and the hand that he was holding out towards her were dusted with sand.

'Look what I found,' he said. In his palm lay a small twig, peaty brown in colour, ancient-looking.

She put her fingers round it, felt its smoothness, looked up into his face with a shock. 'Bone?'

'A finger, I think.' And he jabbed it at her as if in reprimand.

A few days later, Maggie was standing in a queue at the shop and realised that the woman two ahead of her, tipped squint by her loaded basket, was Nora. Maggie was surprised to see the tiny shuffling steps she took as the queue moved forward. She wore flat shoes, round-toed like old-fashioned children's sandals, making it look as if something was wrong with her feet.

Nora didn't appear to have noticed her, but when Maggie left the shop, she found Nora facing the door. Maggie smiled and greeted her, hesitated between going straight to her bicycle and stopping to chat.

'How's it going?' Nora asked.

Maggie wasn't sure what she meant. 'Fine, thanks,' she said, suddenly fearing that Nora knew about the trip to the church and was about to challenge her.

'He's behaving, is he, the lad?' Nora asked with a lip-sticked smile, sunlight flashing on her amber curls.

'Oh, yes,' Maggie said.

'Not getting into places he shouldn't be?'

Maggie thought of the possible danger he'd been in but bluffed, 'Just, you know, drawing away.'

'Aye, well, he'll like that. Always has,' Nora nodded.

'Did he mention the competition?' Maggie had been meaning to phone Nora to remind her about the form, but something had held her back.

Nora looked vague. 'I think he mentioned one, aye.'

'For young cartographers. What did you think? He's got a great map to enter – the one he did for school.'

Nora passed her shopping bag from one hand to the other and Maggie noticed that her nails were perfectly manicured and painted brilliant red.

'I don't recall the details,' Nora said.

'But you're happy for him to enter?'

'If he wants to, aye.'

Maggie breathed more easily but Nora made no further offer. 'The form needs your signature, that's the only thing.'

'Okay.'

'Deadline's any day now.'

'Right you are.'

Maggie heard no conviction in the mother's reply. 'I'll help him with the map of course, it's just the actual entry form.' Maggie paused. 'If he's going to have a chance of a prize.'

Nora laughed then.

There seemed nothing more she could do or say. They said their goodbyes. She stared after Nora, transfixed by her wind-up toy motion. She looked ridiculous, and it seemed to prove her an unsuitable mother for a light-footed boy who moved so effortlessly on any terrain; elf and fish and circus performer.

When Maggie got home, she went online and printed out the form again. The map had to be submitted as an A4 copy. Maggie didn't tell Trothan what she was doing when he came in that afternoon in case it got him into trouble at home.

She borrowed from his pile of papers the original map he'd drawn for the school Open Evening, made a high resolution scan of it and returned it before he could notice.

When she printed from the JPEG later, she was pleased with the way the child's naïve drawing compressed into something neat and coherent.

Then she completed the form. 'Trothan Gilbertson', she wrote, and her own address. She toyed with 'c/o' and decided that it would be inconsistent, completing her own name, signature and date, agreeing that this was 'all the child's own work and that he was under twelve years of age.'

Finally, next to the box for 'Relationship to child', she wrote: 'MOTHER'. It was a necessary untruth; a made-up truth. A warm breeze quivered up from her stomach to animate her hand as she wrote. She put both sheets in a rigid A4 envelope. The sight of the envelope neatly addressed and propped on her table ready for posting the next day made her feel she had come of age.

ELEVEN

It was mid-June when a spring tide inundated the beach, pushing Maggie almost into the grass of the dunes where the sand was soft and difficult to walk on. She laboured and watched her feet. The sky was clear, the air warm, but the emptiness of the place was odd for a summer afternoon, as if human life had been deliberately excluded. It felt a little to Maggie as if she were trespassing.

She reckoned that the tide must be at its peak now; at its point of stillness before retreat. The wind seemed to die and the waves subdue.

As she walked, whispery fragments, silent and white, seemed to be shepherding her from above, just out of her direct sight. She was sure that if she turned and looked at them, they would vanish. She just walked slightly faster. They retained their distance from her, dancing between her arc of vision and her blind spot.

A burn poured out from the dunes about halfway along the beach. She was always curious to see how it engineered its course to the sea. Sometimes it had cut one deep, swaying channel with squared-off, cliff-like edges, and sometimes it parted and re-parted, forming a wide area of shallow tributaries almost like a delta, meaning that you could keep your shoes on to cross it. But with this high tide, it issued straight and deep from a cut in the dunes.

She took off her shoes to cross, looking down at where to place each foot in the rush of sea-seeking water. Somewhere above her head, shrieks floated. She took little notice of them, pressed on with the suck and sink of her feet in the piranha-biting cold. But then she became aware of a change of tone, of frantic bird calls closing in on her. She glanced up. An angular white bird was silhouetted directly above her against the blue sky, its tail fanned out. The wing-quiver that held it in this hover was so imperceptible it gave the bird a threatening power. It was too close, too white, too much focussed on her – the only person on the beach. It dipped a wing, flicked back to level.

As she stepped out of the burn onto the warm dry sand, a mob converged to hang over her. A shriek pierced the air close to her head, and something carved arrow-fast past her with a shock of sharp white feather. She ducked, but another came. She dropped to a crouch, flicked a glance upwards to the flotilla of white forms, thin and ghostlike against the blue sky, tails tightened into angry points and wings like blades. Some were floating low and close to her, others backing them up from a height.

From the corner of her eye, she saw one driving towards her forehead, fan-tailed in its attack. She ducked again but felt the sting of contact, a raw tear on her forehead. Beak or claw. Her hand came away bloody.

She rose slightly, transferring her shoes to one hand so that she could use the free hand as a defence and stepped forward.

Immediately something assaulted her from behind, scuffling her hair. A screech blasted in her ears.

As if under fire in a war-zone she ran bent at the waist, stumbling, hands protecting her head. Her feet scrabbled through sand which blasted up into her eyes and ears, scratching at her. She nearly fell, aware of pursuit by a chorus of icy shrieks. She ran faster. When she finally fell, sprawled with one cheek against sand, she heard her own gasped breathing, but at least the sky had quietened.

She stayed there in the body-shaped dent she'd made, still except for her hands, which pumped at palmfuls of sand. The sight of blood wiped from her face to her hand drove a memory through her. The mother's lips, forehead, cheeks bloodied from kissing the bundle of clothes draped in her lap as she sat in the middle of the road. Maggie had watched as the white dots on the child's red shoes had gradually been erased. Her life flooding out.

'You should wear a hard hat or at least take an umbrella at this time of year,' Graham said. He'd sat her down on the bench outside the Centre and was dabbing at her forehead with moist cotton wool from the first aid kit. She'd seen in the mirror how the red scratch was raised and weeping.

'Ouch.' The antiseptic cream stung.

'It'll be the Arctic ones,' Graham said. 'Vicious buggers when they're protecting their nests. Terns. You were lucky.'

'Lucky?'

'Haven't nested on this beach for quite a few years. They're our most distinguished summer visitors.'

It vaguely pleased her that they were not from here; that it was not the place attacking her, but its immigrants.

'Okay.' Graham looked into her face to assess his handiwork, then frowned slightly. 'You're not going to cry, are you?'

A slab in her throat suddenly told her she might.

'You've had a tetanus jag?' he sat down next to her.

She nodded.

'Come on,' Graham slapped her knee. 'You'll be needing a whisky, then.'

There was quite a crowd in the pub this time. Some of the men looked like they'd been here a while, red-faced, perhaps from the farm and other outdoor jobs. The Butcher and Dounreay-man were in the same positions at the bar as if they'd not moved since Maggie had been there with Carol. The two men greeted her and Graham when they came in.

'Still not on holiday?' The Butcher nudged his drinking partner. 'Remember the Map Lady?'

She inwardly squirmed at the title, but grinned back at them. 'Still doesn't feel quite like a holiday,' she said.

He dabbed a finger at his forehead and her wound smarted in response.

'Altercation with a bird,' she said.

A voice piped up from the other end of the bar: 'Archie'll know all about that, eh?' Approval shook around the smirking heads.

'Take no notice,' he said, swatting them away good-humouredly. 'I'm Archie, by the way.'

They shook hands.

Graham drank orange juice. Maggie drank whisky. Three, maybe four, as they sat at a table in the corner. She breathed more easily now. When Graham went off to the loo before his long drive home, she sat, pleasantly soporific, looking around the bar as if she were invisible.

Behind her a group of three men were speaking with heads drawn close over a table. When she glanced back, one of them appeared to be laying out a map amongst the pints and the beer mats, drawing with great fat fingers dipped in beer. She wondered if they were making some kind of business deal. There were snatches of nonsensical conversation.

'Found a metatarsal in the wall of his new ensuite.'

'New kind of building material, eh?'

There were great gobby guffaws of laughter.

'Got phalanges muddled up with his flanges, eh?'

'Them bones, them bones, them dry bones.'

When Graham returned, she knew it was time to leave, but the seat seemed to tug her down into a sort of whisky-dulled paralysis. 'Thanks, by the way,' she said. 'For rescuing me from those sky-witches.'

'All part of the service,' he said. 'Can't leave distressed damsels in a heap on the beach. They might get disappeared along with the sand.'

She nodded, dazed and almost tearful again. His eyes seemed to remain fixed on her.

'Ach, they're just wee birdies,' he said. 'Nothing to get upset about. They'll be leaving soon anyway, once their eggs are hatched. Off 11,000 miles to their next summer.'

She swiped her nose against her sleeve.

'It's not just the terns, is it?' he said.

She sniffed. Stared ahead. 'I don't know what you mean.'

'That's getting to you?'

She chewed her lip. 'Just, you know, other stuff.' She heard the drunkenness in her own voice, batted away the conversation with a hand and moved to the front of her seat, ready to stand up.

'It's like you're haunted by something,' he said.

'Hunted?'

'Well that too, maybe, but it's my accent.' He spelt it out then.

She knotted her hands together. Found nothing to say.

'Come on, I'll give you a lift home.'

When she opened her mouth to object, he said, 'The bike'll be fine here, round the back.'

There was sunlight, weak, very early morning sunlight, and there was pain. Something had woken her, a click as if someone had closed a door somewhere. The pain was a dull beat in her head, was pulsing in an ankle sprained years before, was in her stiff shoulders as usual. She closed her eyes. Slept again.

There was flickering behind her eyelids. Birds outside and trees, the sky wheeling around. A memory of standing on the pavement in what seemed broad daylight despite the dark bar, the whisky, with Graham saying, 'And ten days yet to the solstice.'

She remembered that the bike was propped against the back wall of the hotel, or stolen by now, perhaps.

And she remembered lying on this bed, the fine long night stretching way after midnight. She remembered hearing the sea and the rumble of an engine somewhere going backwards and forwards in short bursts. Just lying there, tolerating, listening, drifting towards a sort of sleep.

She rolled over in bed, put her hand to her forehead. The tern's wound was smarting and crusty with blood. Her watch said nearly eight o'clock. It had already been light for five hours. She pulled herself up to sitting. Her bedroom curtains were open. She'd slept with all that sunlight flooding onto her. Rooks were circling above the high green tops of the trees.

She got up, moving tentatively. She would make tea and work out things from there.

In the kitchen her head pulsed and thudded, sounds that almost seemed to pound in from the hall or the sitting room. She grabbed at the remains of yesterday's loaf and sawed a great hunk off, smeared it with peanut butter and tore at it with her teeth. When it reached her stomach it was sweet and instantly healing.

She carried a cup of tea towards the sitting room door and as she opened it shocked half the contents of her mug across the floor. Trothan was sitting at her table, drawing. He looked up through the tangled fringe, coy and smiling. There was something about his posture that looked hastily arranged though, as if he'd been up to something else and was now posing with the map for her benefit. A stool that was usually tucked in at the far end of the table had been moved and was standing close by him. When she didn't speak, he resumed his drawing.

She put down her mug, rested her palms on the table, spread them, facing the boy and looking over his map. Irritation drew itself up to a monstrous height inside her. Why was he intruding on her hang-over?

'What are you doing here?' she asked. 'At this time on a Saturday morning?'

'I'm doing the bit at Dwarwick harbour,' he said, pointing at a sketch. His pencil continued its scratching.

She scanned the room to see if anything was out of place, to see what he might have been up to.

'Do your parents know you're here?'

He nodded unconvincingly.

'Shall I just give them a call to check?'

No response.

'And why's there sand all over the table?' She saw the grains glinting, a loose drift of them, that she brushed up with her hand into a small pyramid.

He shrugged.

'Trothan. Look at me.'

He didn't. She could hear his breath as he hatched lines across a building on his drawing. Flick, flick, flick, with the pencil.

She grabbed the pencil out of his hand, making a sweeping black mark across the bay from Dwarwick harbour as if it was the determined route of a pipeline.

'Listen.' She leant in, hating him now as much as she'd done when he terrorised her in the woods. Had it been him? Her voice was terse, trembling. 'You'd better be telling me the truth.' She wheeled away and then flung back at him: 'Was it you that built that snowman in my garden?'

His eyes were large, dark beads staring up at her with surprise.

'Come on,' she pressed back in on him, raising her voice. She grabbed across the table at his arm, gripped it hard, shook it, saying loudly now. 'Come on.'

She saw a childish flicker in his eyes. Then a twitch beside his mouth dragged downwards in his strange, ugly, flat face. A single tear rose from his right eye, coursed down his cheek while his mouth pursed in an attempt at control. The child was crying. She had made him cry. With it came a horrible reminder of Frank's face as he told her he was leaving. She'd been unable to reach out to him or to feel anything other than the certainty that she deserved it.

She dropped his arm. 'Trothan, Trothan,' she said gently, and moved to his side of the table, kneeling next to him, a hand to his arm. The small body was silently heaving, hands now up to his eyes, covering them.

'I'm sorry, I'm sorry,' she whispered. 'It's all right. I'm just crabby this morning, and I was surprised to see you.'

She recalled so well herself that dreadful agony of being wrong as a child, of being the brunt of anger, of being shaken out of her security and sense of love. Her pain now was knowing both sides of it.

She felt an impulse to reach out with her body, to hug him. It seemed so natural, but she held back, looked up into his hair-tangled face and smiled. 'I'm going to make you a lovely mug of milky chocolate, just as you like it.'

She withdrew to the kitchen to let him recover his composure; to recover her own. He was vulnerable, just as she'd suspected.

When she returned with the chocolate, she was relieved to see that he was drawing again and she didn't pursue her questioning.

He looked up at her, staring and silent for a moment. 'Did something happen to your head?'

She nodded. 'A bird happened.'

From a distance, over Trothan's shoulder, she saw what he was sketching. A body in freefall. It looked as if it was twisting in the air. Its head was pointing down to the bottom of the page, short arms flung outwards as it plummeted, legs apparently wrapped around each other in a swivel; a downward pirouette. She thought of angels falling to earth; the short arms their wings.

Then she saw flecks scattered across the page above it. She moved closer. Bubbles. She realised that the substance of the page wasn't air, but water. The body was elegant in its flight, controlled, and not falling at all, but swimming. Not even swimming, but almost dancing down through it. And it wasn't human, but a seal.

She noticed then the second one swimming across the page below it, arching its back so that its stomach curved towards the bottom of the page, head and tail pointing upwards. And there was a dark eye, a wide nostril and whiskers.

'You've been to the Sea Life Centre, haven't you?' she said. 'Seen seals swimming through the glass?'

He gave a small start, jolted from his concentration, and turned his head slightly. 'No.'

'TV, then.'

He shook his head.

'So how do you know how they look?'

'Just out of my head.'

What he always said.

'Do you know,' he said. 'There's a dead cow washed up on Peadie Sands, and no one's supposed to go there.'

'A dead cow?'

'All smelly. Right here, it is,' and he pointed with his finger on the map.

She suddenly recalled the dead seal and its raw, round wound. 'Where did it come from?'

He shrugged. 'Fell off a cliff, I suppose. Or swam from Orkney.' He let out a squeaky laugh. 'Do you think they do that? Swim all the way from Orkney?'

They both laughed. She put the hot chocolate down next to him, went to stand behind him, observing over his shoulder new details on his map. A ship sailed into the bay with sails billowing. It wasn't Viking in shape, more like a galley – a slave ship.

Their intimate little boat was re-stabilising after a storm, and she put a hand on each of his shoulders, felt the heat coming up into her palms, put her fingers like a comb to his hair, straggling and damp at the back, sparkling with sand.

A movement through the window caught her eye. Something passed the first window; something substantial. She stiffened, took her hands off the boy, watched the second window. Trothan continued working, head down.

Sure enough, at the second window, the sun caught on the bright back of Nora's head. As if in slow motion, she turned towards the room, her eyes locking on to Maggie's, taking in the scene.

Maggie remained frozen as the woman tottered around the corner of the building, hands on the wall to steady her steps. Her intrusion was now inevitable. Maggie felt caught out somehow, but caught doing what? What she was doing was entirely normal and within her rights with a child who needed attention and affection from her.

Nora's bulky outline loomed at the glass door now, hands hanging by her sides. She made no attempt to knock or open the door, and Maggie stayed momentarily where she was, so that they stood facing each other with Trothan oblivious between them.

Finally Maggie said very quietly, 'Trothan, your mother's come for you.' And she gestured at Nora to come in.

He looked up, saw Nora and waved, and then was pushing his chair back into Maggie, packing up his things and heading for the door.

Nora took his bag. 'You have said thank you, have you?'

Trothan turned and waved and Maggie's gut twisted with disappointment at his eagerness. It was as if this was a normal ritual of childminder and parent. As if it had been arranged. But Nora's arrival felt like it had been engineered to force an unwelcome meeting of two worlds which should remain apart.

'You haven't left anything here?' Nora said looking down

with a slight frown to Trothan. He passed her and she looked at Maggie, seemed to appeal to her with the same question. Maggie glanced along the table where he'd been sitting and shook her head.

Nora nodded but still hesitated, as if there was something more to say, searching the place with her eyes.

'He's got his map,' Maggie said. 'And the drawing things. I always let him borrow them.' Maggie was struggling to understand what she was looking for.

'We've got to get going,' Nora said. 'Off to my sister's. Thought I might find him here.'

Then Trothan's disappearing back seemed to catch Nora's attention and she said goodbye, closed the door, pursued him around the corner of the cottage with her strange jerky gait.

Not long afterwards Maggie heard an engine start up in the lane.

TWELVE

Later that morning, sitting reading the paper in a break from her computer, she became aware of a draught trickling down her neck. She looked up and for the first time noticed the loft hatch immediately above the table. It was a small square in the ceiling, and the lid was obviously just a simple board. It was propped at an angle, not seated properly, revealing a triangle of darkness through which cold air was descending.

The ceiling was low and she realised she could easily reach it by standing on the robust table. She took off her shoes. The table felt gritty under her soles, and looking down, she saw that a scattering of sand was catching the sunlight. Trothan's pile.

It would have been a simple exercise just to re-seat the lid so that the loft was sealed again and draught-free, but curiosity sent her to get a head-torch.

In her previous house, Maggie had avoided the loft. It was Frank or the plumber or loft insulator who went up there. But an occasion had come when she was alone with a leaking pipe and it was unavoidable. When she discovered some alien objects lurking in the dark, left there by previous occupants, she'd been shocked into a sudden sense that the house wasn't quite her own and never had been.

She put the stool onto the table top and when she stood on it, she had enough height to see inside. The torch batteries were failing and only illuminated things slightly; bare rafters slanting away across one side of the roof and yellow fibreglass wool bubbling up between the joists. She checked the corners of the loft, straining till her eyes adjusted; the first, second, third were empty. There were cobwebs, a musty odour, but no mysterious boxes, treasure chests, rocking horses. She was quite satisfied, ready to slide the lid back into place and descend again. But then she saw into the fourth corner. In the faint light something bulky lay, its shape and form distinctly animal-like.

Pushing the lid to one side, she levered herself up on her arms until she was perched on the edge of the hatch. She swivelled onto hands and knees, facing the thing at a distance, and then she stood up as much as the roof height allowed her to, feeling the crackly rub of cobweb and sun-dried flies in her hair as well as the bump of her skull on the roof. Bending from the waist, she shuffled forwards, putting her hands onto the leaning rafters to steady herself. She tried to imagine the joists as planks rather than tight-ropes. Focussing on that, she inched clumsily towards the corner, feeling the fragility of the surface beneath her as if she was completely exposed, as if she could see down to her dining table, the sofa, and her pile of magazines.

It wasn't until she was practically on top of the beached thing that she even looked at it, so concerned was she with the placement of her feet. She stood still, centred herself with a deep breath and directed the weak torch beam downwards. There was a sudden shock of fur, sleek-looking against loose skin. She had time to see that it was the size of a large dog. And then the torch died.

Paralysed by darkness, her heart battering in her chest, she concentrated on stilling her breathing. The faint babble of Radio Four voices drifted up through the loft hatch. The smell of something outdoorish was strong here. She dropped back down to hands and knees, finding the exact line of the joist, and inched her right hand forward; repulsion as strong as the wish to find it. And then her hand butted up against something soft, firm, immobile.

Her finger traced one-way and then stuttered the other way against the grain of the fur. It was definitely fur, somehow simultaneously silky and coarse. She let her hand roam, finding the edges of a skin which stretched for several feet across the joists. It was folded like a huge coat and cold to the touch.

She attempted to scoop the thing towards herself and reluctantly it came. She pulled it until it lay heavily across her knees and then began very slowly to move backwards, one hand holding it and the other clinging tightly to the single joist. She knew when she'd reached the hatch by the increased light and the knock of her toe against the abandoned lid. She scooped up the skin in one arm and twisting towards the hatch, threw it so that, dragged by its own weight, it trickled downwards. She heard a series of thuds and smacks and then it landed below, bringing a coffee mug smashing onto the floor from the table. She lowered herself down after it.

It had ended up draped over a dining room chair, fur outwards, its form fluid and cat-like. It was grey and six-foot or so long, the shape of the long, tapering tail still distinct and the head laid out like a two-dimensional plan with huge holes for eye sockets and puckers where whiskers had been.

She wished she didn't have to face this alone. It brought to mind a horse's head left in a bed in *The Godfather*.

She phoned Richard. There were still outstanding graphics to discuss anyway. Once that was done, she asked: 'What would you think if you found an animal skin in your loft?'

'I'd think, "That's where Kitty disappeared to five years ago".'

'A cat?'

'Abandoned me, as all women like to, never saw hide nor hair of her again. At least, not until her hide turned up in your hypothetical loft.'

'This still has fur though. It is, was, a seal.'

'Might be worth something,' he said. 'Isn't there a big illegal market in sealskins from Norway?'

'Right. So someone's hiding it there until the price is right?'

'Maybe,' he said. 'In a rented house, anyone could have left it there. You'd better find an expert.'

'Graham,' she said. 'I'll ask Graham.'

'Who's he?'

'The local ranger.'

'A Lone Ranger?'

Was he digging? 'Shut up, Tonto.'

She heard him sigh.

She made coffee and sat opposite the skin, didn't read or even look out of the window. She wondered what to do with it. Eventually she picked up the phone to Sally, who at least knew the house.

'I'm thinking of putting some boxes of stuff that I don't really need in the loft,' she said once pleasantries were over. 'Would that be alright?'

'Well, you might find it a bit hard because there's no boards laid.'

'Oh, really. Do you have anything stored up there yourselves?'

'No, no.'

'Or might a past tenant have left anything?'

'Your predecessors were only in a few months while they had some work done on their own house. I doubt they used it. Well you'll know that anyway, as you...'

Maggie interrupted: 'So it's empty?'

'Yes, and to be honest, we'd prefer to keep it like that.'

She put the phone down and continued to stare at her new companion.

On the way back from the village where she'd been to collect her bicycle, she passed Debbie's salon. All her aches and pains from the roughing up she'd taken the previous day suddenly seemed to demand a massage.

'You've been in the wars then,' Debbie said when she saw the red weal across Maggie's forehead.

Maggie put up her hand, touched the wound. 'A bird,' she said.

Debbie nodded but didn't look like she believed it.

She was perfectly polite, but there was something brisker in Debbie's manner this time, at odds with the busty, over ripe body. She clearly couldn't hold in all her words though. Questions started bubbling up as the massage began to loosen them both with its oily, aromatic spell.

'So, have you made many friends?'

A hook dangling from the line of the question, a short pause, then: 'I hear you've been giving the Gilbertson boy some extra tuition.'

Maggie muttered into the towel against her mouth and nothing more was said.

They went through the same ritual as before with the towels

pulled up over her. She was left lying face down to recover, trying to empty her mind.

She heard a door open on the other side of the partition, a man's voice accompanied by a frantic scrabbling, claws scratching on the hard floor. Debbie's high surprised voice remonstrating.

'Sit, Brutus,' she heard from the man.

Some more protesting noises from Debbie.

'Meet Brutus. My new assistant.' Gruff. Loud.

More scrabbles, Debbie murmuring now.

'Steady,' the man said, then louder, threatening: 'Steady.'

Debbie's voice again. A question this time.

'For up there, the church.'

Another question.

'To scare off they snooping bastards, eh, Brutus.'

This time the scrabbling was accompanied by the sound of things scattering on the floor and then Debbie's voice rising, her words now discernible: 'Get him out of here, he's too big.'

The door opened and the male voice faded. 'Fuck's sake, Brutus. You'll pull my arm out its socket.'

The door closed and peace resumed.

Maggie pictured a kind of thorny stockade going up around the church.

As soon as she got home she went to lie down on the bed but woke at a noise. She jumped up, barefoot and slightly shaky, and walked through to the main room. At the glass door, she saw two figures in peaked caps and black combat jackets, a stripe of checked fluorescent across each chest. Police. They must've knocked.

'What's happened?' she asked, flinging open the door.

'Nothing to worry about. This is PC Anderson and I'm PC

Small, Community Police', the man said. 'Sorry to disturb you.'

Maggie couldn't help noticing how ridiculous they looked side-by-side as she waited, still breathing her dreams, to hear what they'd come for. He was tall, dark and thin, and had to stoop to come through the door when Maggie invited them in – PC Small. Anderson was short, blonde and wide.

The presence of authority figures agitated in Maggie both a juvenile and a submissive streak; simultaneously giggly and guilty. She went to make coffee. It gave her a few minutes; the flood of caffeine settling her back into daylight and adulthood.

They seemed reluctant to speak at first, as if waiting for her.

'It was probably time to come and say hello anyway.' PC Small – the tall one – was leaning against the sealskin draped over the back of his seat, but not apparently noticing it.

'Oh?' She felt confused. What did that 'anyway' refer to? An innate sense of guilt gathered momentum.

'You've not long moved to the area, is that right?'

'Three or four months,' she said.

Small nodded. Anderson, her hands cupped around one black-trousered knee, was leaning back, gazing around the room.

'You'll be finding your way around, getting to know a few folk? It's a friendly wee place, I hope you've found.'

She nodded.

'Takes a few years to get familiar with all its characters.' Small turned to his accomplice and they both laughed. 'Most people rub along fine. We just get the odd crime to sort out – mostly untaxed cars, that kind of thing.'

So that was it. She glanced through the window to the Volvo with the lapsed tax disc. 'I haven't been using my car, not really, that's why...'

'I assume you know the Gilbertsons? They're friends of

yours?' Anderson cut her short.

She looked up sharply. Had something happened? 'Trothan, the boy, yes.'

They looked at her silently.

'Would you mind describing your connection to Trothan?'

Maggie resisted the irritating memory this brought of Carol's line of questioning. 'Friend, I suppose.'

'Friend?' Both looked at her quizzically.

'Well, I've been helping him. I'm a cartographer and he's very interested in maps. I'm helping him.'

The man continued. 'And where do you help him?'

'He comes here.'

She felt rather than saw their raised eyebrows.

'When does he come here? How often?'

'Several times a week.' She didn't want to admit that it was daily.

'An arrangement with his parents, I imagine?' Small said. 'Childminding?'

She struggled. 'Well, not officially or anything. But you could describe it like that. Working parents and so on.'

She sweated and her hands were hot. She sat on them. It was as if the officers saw something slightly distasteful in her intent towards the boy.

'It's just that we've had a few comments about his wanderings.'

'Oh?'

'Not quite as strong as complaints, but almost.'

Maggie frowned. 'He's pretty harmless, isn't he? A child?'

'That's not really the point. People sometimes see it as trespass.'

'Who's been complaining? About where?' Maggie challenged.

'I should make it clear,' Small continued, 'that this is an informal visit, advisory, there won't be any records kept.'

'Advising whom?'

'Just to let you know,' Anderson chipped in. 'So you're in the picture too.'

Maggie looked from one to the other. 'So who's been complaining?'

'He's been seen at various places, including the Gatehouse Lodge, and some building sites near the village. It's been suggested to us that you might have been encouraging the boy.'

'I have indeed. He's an excellent draughtsman.'

'In his explorations,' Anderson corrected.

She recalled something she'd said to Trothan just the week before about a gap on his map: 'Do you think the early mapmakers would have left blank spaces on the map rather than march on past every PRIVATE sign?' She'd talked to him again about Timothy Pont walking the whole wild, roadless kingdom and having to deal with hostile people, being robbed and harassed but never allowing himself to despair or to stop his sketching. Did that make her responsible? She thought then of Rab McNicholl's words about 'they snooping bastards'. Perhaps she and Trothan had been seen at the church the other evening.

'Quite apart from anything else, these are dangerous places,' Small said.

'Shouldn't it be his parents you're talking to, then?'

'As long as you stick to public places, you'll be fine.'

'"You"?'

'Sorry?'

'You said "you". I thought we were talking about Trothan.'

Small put down his coffee cup and got up, unfolding himself towards the ceiling. Anderson hastily slurped the rest of hers, and followed suit.

'Thanks for the coffee,' Small said, giving her a polite smile.

Maggie remained sitting for a moment. She wasn't quite sure what she was being accused of or who was issuing the warning.

As they stood there, looking at her, she heard the dry crunch of tyres on the gravel. Through the window she saw Jim's refrigerated van turn into the drive behind the police car, lurch to a stop and reverse.

'Expecting a delivery?' Small asked, grinning.

Anderson's radio started to crackle. She indicated the door and let herself out.

Small put his hat on, was looming, apparently leaving, when he turned in the doorway. 'Do you mind me asking why you moved here?'

'To live,' her lips felt rigid against her teeth.

'Wouldn't have anything to do with Lizzy Ginner, would it?'

When she didn't answer, he left.

Winded, she saw him shut the door, pass all the windows, and heard the car reverse out of the drive and rumble off along the lane. She sat still for a long time not quite able to remove herself from the Oxford street he had evoked, lined with parked cars.

Maggie never knew what had transfixed the child; what she had seen on the far side of the road. Perhaps it had simply been a bird pecking at a rowan berry or a cat, resembling the girl's own fat ginger 'Orlando', caught by fear high in the branches of a tree.

The warning had started as a word; the girl's name perhaps. The mother's rebuke. A sharp cry that came clattering in through the open car window.

Maggie had turned the wheel to the right, an impulse to cut

the child off, to squeeze between the gap. The brakes squealed. But the child was moving too fast. Maggie veered left and that was when the car careered into a skid, the driver's wing leading the direction of travel straight down the broken white line.

The mother's word never finishes. Her cry rises on the second syllable. In volume. In pitch. It stretches on, hurtling towards the sound Maggie forever refuses to hear.

THIRTEEN

In the days after Nora came and took him away, Trothan didn't turn up at Flotsam Cottage. Having picked away at her work for months, the first set of atlas proofs were due with Richard in just over a week's time. There was still quite a lot to do. It wasn't that she hadn't taken it seriously, but somehow working out of the office made the whole project seem less real. It was approaching midsummer now, and the extensive daylight seemed to promise scope for long hours of work.

Her graphic to show the expansion of Lagos was only a small fraction of her outstanding work and yet it preoccupied her. The more she read about the city, the more complex the story seemed. Contained by a seafront, comprised of sinking islands and a mainland divided by a many-headed lagoon, the city was said to draw 6,000 new people to live in it daily. She couldn't think of a way to represent its attraction. Despite some developments in water supply, electricity, transport and housing, the infrastructure surely couldn't keep pace. The mesmerised immigrants settled on its peripheries and on the margins of canals and railway lines; teetered on stilts above swamps. They might build homes from driftwood, tin and cardboard or inhabit high rises and work for multinational companies.

She pictured these people vanishing into the fattening giant of the city. It conjured images of a cannibalistic beast from a medieval map; images that had been commonly reserved for the African continent, instilling dark superstition and prejudice in European minds. One contemporary map she'd seen isolated the sixteen districts of the city, and their arrangement suggested a huge animal head – the lagoon its great open mouth, Lagos island its lolling tongue. Agege was the eye; Ifako Ijaye its pricked ear; Eti Osa the long protruding lower jaw. It was tempting to see the city as a devouring beast, cannibalising the rest of Nigeria.

She played God with Google Earth in her attempts to come up with an answer. The lagoon appeared slick grey as if running with oil; the aerial view partially obscured by smog. She wanted to get down there, crackle her feet amongst garbage, feel the squeeze of heat amidst the honking lanes of stationary traffic. But it pixellated into obscurity when she tried to draw too close.

Any kind of opportunity was available there, it seemed from her reading; a chance to be any kind of person. Designer shoes and sunglasses were on offer to village folk, albeit fake ones. Taking a leaf from Trothan's book, she was tempted to depict the city's lure as a Pied Piper, leading multitudes through a doorway in a hillside with a promise of transformation. But the Pied Piper story would be meaningless to Nigerian High School students, as might Greek Sirens.

Richard encouraged her away from explanations of the city's attraction.

'Just find a nice clear way of showing the population growth since the oil boom of the 60s,' he said.

But she knew 'the population growth' was more than facts

and figures, even if there had been any sure ones, and she began to see that the accuracy of a map was more than geographic – it needed to be accurate about hidden and psychological matters too. It needed to spark up imaginations. Lagos remained mysterious and elusive to her. A city that was its own mythical country.

In the first day or two that she dedicated herself to her work, the sealskin's watchful presence distracted her. She decided to put it in the garden out of her sight. Its fur seemed risen and rough when she picked it up. She carried it to the door, but when she saw that it was raining, didn't feel she could abandon it to the elements and so returned it to the chair. The sun shone the next day, and when she put her fingers to the fur it had relaxed into silky softness. She sprang away from it; an animate, living barometer. Left it where it was.

Her work kept her indoors. The threatening visit from the police and all it had stirred up nagged at her. She waited for Trothan to reappear, and when he didn't, she wondered if he was ill. It even crossed her mind that he'd run away. Perhaps the police had given him a ticking off too. If she left the house, she locked the door against intruders, but was anxious that Trothan might arrive when she was out. She left notes for him taped to the door, but they were still there when she got home. She was fairly sure it was simply that Nora was clawing him back.

When Audrey phoned it felt like a small victory. Trothan's map had been randomly picked for the end of year showcase for parents. As Maggie had been helping him with it, would she be willing to do a double act for his five minute presentation?

'We really mean five minutes,' Audrey warned. 'You get your head cut off if it's any longer. I'm sure I can rely on you to keep the lad straight.'

'I'd be delighted,' Maggie said.

'I know they're a bit tedious, these events, but if you could bear it we'd be very grateful.'

Maggie heard it as confirmation of her special place in Trothan's life. 'What about his parents?' she asked.

There was a pause. 'Well, they'll be there, I'm quite sure,' Audrey said.

As if they were proud of him, thought Maggie, but hesitated to put Audrey right.

She'd never had an opportunity for vicarious pride in a child before. Fran and Jamie had always been so protected by their parents that they had been distant to her. And anyway at the particular time that she was with them every weekend, she'd been distant to everything.

Trothan's absence made her anxious about how they'd prepare for the event. She worried about it enough that she fortified herself to phone his parents, but when she did, there was no answer. She visualised his map; what she knew of it. As the process had gone on, he seemed to have become more secretive and she'd seen less and less of it. She longed to ask what yet another sheet of film he'd requested was for; an eighth layer. When she'd last seen him, he hadn't yet started on the composite version of the map. All these uncertainties seemed to add to the more usual stress of a deadline looming for her own work, just the day after the school showcase.

Raising her head more than once at a sound from outside, she looked out of the window to anticipate his approach, and sat down frowning again when there was only an empty path. She wanted to collude with him; to foresee how he would impress Audrey, the school, his parents; and to make sure he wasn't being intimidated out of his explorations.

She made a small loaf most days in breaks from the computer, kneading comfort back into herself, her hands warm in the soft dough, strong on it as she stretched and beat. She used no measures now; mixed dough intuitively. It always made her feel better, especially as it rose into its fleshy mound on a warm windowsill and then filled the house as it baked with its great huff of warm scent.

She fought on to get her work done, snatching sleep between midnight and three a.m. Even then, it was barely dark. And the night sounds continued: the kids in the woods or wherever they were; the young men's roaring cars circling the village; and the heave of mechanical equipment droning from the direction of the bay in the darkest hours. She began to understand the notion of madness that came with a midsummer lack of sleep, the hallucinatory quality of the restless day-night.

All day, each day, making the most of light and a decent spell of weather, the chorus of cement-mixers churned on. She sensed breeze block bungalows rising from the ground almost as if, block for block, they corresponded with the stone cottages crumbling back into the earth. And yet she heard on the radio that house-building across the UK had dropped to the levels of the 1920s.

One afternoon towards the end of her week of concentrated work, she took time out and walked down to the beach. The verges she passed hummed with pollen from meadowsweet and sweet cicely; mauve clover-heads the size of golf balls lined the way. The fields were a haze of buttercup yellow. Curlews burbled above her, stone chats in the gorse chit-chatted, and once she was on the beach, the waves hypnotised. The twin arms of Holborn Head and Dwarwick Head, rather than closing in the bay as they sometimes did, seemed to open wider, revealing an expansive horizon to the Atlantic, the Northwest. It was like an invitation to travel beyond the offing, and she watched ships, toy-like, pioneering their way through the Pentland Firth.

Tourists had arrived. There were motor-homes parked up on the campsite behind the Sandpiper Centre, and cyclists doing the 'end to end' dotted the road in fluorescent jackets.

Graham was busy with visitors when she arrived at the Centre, so she stood at the window watching the bay through binoculars. Voices rose behind her, a tourist remonstrating with him.

'We've been coming here fifteen years and we've never seen this going on before.'

She heard Graham's voice quiet and slow; pacifying.

The other voice came back again: 'But surely it's protected? Surely they can't remove sand from the dunes just like that? Surely someone must be able to stop them.'

'Of course we might like to...' She heard the irritation beginning to prickle in Graham's voice as he explained that it wasn't his responsibility.

She was reminded of what she'd learnt about Lagos, the Lekki district. Sand was being dredged from the seabed to shore up the vulnerable margins of some of the marshy islands. Lavish apartments for the rich were springing up there, built on shifting foundations of corruption. Presumably the sea would demolish them within years. It was obvious. But still the rich were entrusting themselves to a mirage. In turn the moved sand had blocked drainage canals, so that when the rains came, the vegetable market flooded, and small businesses owned by much poorer people had to be abandoned. Her incomplete dealings with Lagos niggled at her now, and she wanted to shake them off. Richard had told her again, quite firmly this time, that such detail was irrelevant. But she couldn't quite let it go.

Maggie turned to see the man with binoculars round his neck stomp away without a satisfactory answer. Graham watched him go with arms stiff at his sides, heaved a sigh and then joined her at the window.

He was as mystified as her about the sealskin. 'Can't help there, I'm afraid. Unless it was someone's trophy.'

She was disappointed not to have found an explanation; still unsure what to do with the thing. 'Perhaps I'll just shove it back in the loft,' she said.

They looked out on the beach again.

'You should get yourself out to Dunnet Head,' he said. 'The guillemots've got their young now. Precious single bairns.'

She thought of Trothan and felt another little twist of anxiety at his absence. She'd half-hoped she might hear something of him when she was out. But he barely seemed to touch anyone else's lives.

'You're alright now, are you – after the tern attack and that?' Graham asked.

'Oh that,' she said, an involuntary lock in her breath.

'And the whisky,' he teased.

'It was you made me drink it,' she said.

'Only because I thought you were about to cry.'

'What?' She half-protested, turned away to the window.

'Right, let's see what else is out there to attack you,' he said, standing by her side and picking up the binoculars.

By the time she got back to the village it was hot, the humidity reaching a peak now, and moisture clouds were pressing low on the horizon. People were out in shorts and singlets, sunburned, eating ice creams. Boys rode past on their ridiculous low-saddled bikes. In the playpark, a cluster of small girls sported pinkened skin. She was surprised when two of them turned on the climbing frame and waved at her as she passed, smiling. She half-looked over her shoulder to see who they'd seen behind her. 'Hello Maggie,' one of them called out. She waved back, realising she must have met them on her visits to the school.

A police car slunk down the main street and induced in Maggie a guilty flinch. She went into the shop for a couple of things and then on an impulse, instead of turning for home, she turned into the grid of streets, touring them systematically until she found the one with the right name.

It was a street of single-storey quarriers' cottages. Each short, front garden had a narrow gravel path leading to the front door across a lawn. She walked until she found their house number. A builder's van was parked outside the gate. It wasn't Rab McNicholl's but a blue one from Thurso. The house was prickling with scaffolding and two men straddled the roof, hammering new sarking boards across the bare frame. A radio was bellowing summer pop songs into the sky and a voice accompanied it in yelps and high notes that were abbreviated by the regular beating of two hammers.

She stopped, stared. The front door stood wide open and builders' tools and stacks of slates were dumped right in front of it. The house betrayed no occupants.

She pushed the gate open and stood in the centre of the path.

'*I need you more than want you,*' wailed the younger man along with Glen Campbell.

'Excuse me,' she shouted up, repeating it when the song continued.

Eventually the banging paused on both ends of the roof and

the two men peered down at her, legs braced in front of them.

'The Gilbertsons?' she asked.

'We've put them out, darling.' The older man smiled down at her.

'Put them out?' She had a picture of eviction, of rent arrears. 'Where have they gone?'

The men looked at each other. 'To her sister's, I think.'

'Where's that?'

The younger man named a place she'd never heard of and the older one added, 'Far side of Thurso.'

Maggie put her hand to her head. Trothan in a new house, a new school, totally removed from the area.

'Put a note in the house if you like, they'll get it when they're back.'

Relief flooded her. 'They've not moved out then?'

'We've only put them out while we do this. They don't think much about his singing, eh?' The older man laughed.

The younger one resumed his hammering, and, more quietly, his singing.

'When are they back?' she called, but was not heard.

It was dark in the house by contrast to the brilliance of the day and her eyes took a moment to adjust. She walked straight into a small sitting room with a sofa and two matching armchairs in a traditional floral print. The room seemed crowded with furniture; gingham, the smell of artificial air-freshener. There was a well-trodden sense of people going in and out, wearing the dark carpet thin towards the door where traces of sand scattered from the threshold. A fake wood-burning stove stood in a fireplace. A shelf behind it was decorated with a few ornaments, some books and a TV.

On the wall there were photos. She moved closer. A small

baby wrapped in a white blanket with a solemn, elfin face and huge brown eyes. Trothan holding his mother's hand on the front path, a small red rucksack on his back – the first day at school, she imagined. Another outside Edinburgh Castle. Always Trothan with his mother or father, never anyone else, never any friends or wider family, the photo always taken by one of them.

It seemed a normal, traditional house; just small. There would be nowhere to lay out a map to work on it; there was no computer or laptop visible. She found the bathroom off the living room. It was decorated with seahorse tiles, bright soaps that gushed strawberry scent, a fluffy bath mat. Everything was in its place, as if the house had been prepared for an absence. A house that felt private and contained, holding the lives of three people in a contented balance with each other.

She registered a sense of disappointment. She'd expected to find some evidence of discord or negligence but wasn't sure how that would have looked anyway. Discarded chip wrappers on the floor or dangerous things left lying about? But then she thought, perhaps a child left excessively to himself would make a home within a home in his bedroom.

The hammering was still coming regularly from above. She glanced down the path through the open door, then moved quickly. She soon found it – a small room with a single bed and a jungle-themed duvet cover. Fishes dangled from a mobile, spinning in sunlight. There was a shelf of books – dinosaurs featured, just like in her nephew Jamie's room. There were childish, but accomplished drawings of boats and animals on the wall. Apart from that, there was none of the usual children's paraphernalia of TV, computer, boy band posters. There was no sign either of the roll of maps or Rotring pens. He must have taken them. He must still be working on the map.

The bed sank beneath her and she felt herself sucked down by tiredness. She would rest, just for a minute or two, somewhere she felt safe and secure. Unable to battle it any longer, she leant her head down onto the pillow. The salty scent of Trothan. Faint but distinct. She closed her eyes despite the open door, her trespass, the persistent hammering and singing descending the pitch of the roof above her. It would beat out time until the two men descended and might discover that she was still here, sleeping with her feet on the floor.

FOURTEEN

The Wednesday of the school showcase was another blue-skied scorcher. Late in the afternoon, Maggie went for a walk on the beach, lay down for a moment in the sun and woke to find that a bank of greasy cloud was spilling over Dunnet Head, oozing down towards the beach; a blanket of the infamous haar wrought by cool sea air colliding with the hot land. It moved stealthily, covering the village of Dunnet except for the white tower of the church which pierced through it. Feeling its chill effect in anticipation, she stood up and brushed the sand from her hair.

At home, she considered what to wear. She could feel sunburn pulsing down one side of her face; the effect of her brief sleep on the beach. Despite the cool fog now enveloping the village, she chose a summer dress. But when she put it on the neckline exposed a white scallop of chest. She considered changing but instead she retrieved the cornflower blue scarf that had hung over the hall mirror since she'd arrived. She draped it around her neck and shoulders to mediate her skin colours and then peered at herself in the mirror. She found an ancient tube of blocking foundation which she rubbed onto the red flash on her left cheek and the flaming bulb of one nostril, put on sandals, and found a handbag into which she put a notebook and pen. Snatching a final glance in the mirror she rescued lipstick from the depths of her bag, dabbed some on and then plunged out of the door.

She hadn't expected the school hall to be quite so packed. Two swathes of seats had been set out with an aisle down the centre. The parents seemed to be treating it almost as a prize-giving ceremony; there were frocks and even the occasional hat.

Audrey button-holed her as soon as she came in, handing her a piece of paper. 'Here's the questions I'd suggest.'

'For Trothan?' Maggie asked. 'You know we've not had a chance to plan this? He's been away.'

'I know. He's not been at school for a few days either.' Audrey was twitchy, looking around, perhaps ticking off a mental list of people she had to speak to. 'It'll be fine, just show the map and get him to answer the questions. Haven't had a chance to look at it myself. He finished it while he's been away apparently, but Mrs Burt's uploaded a scan onto the laptop so he can project it.'

'The whole map?'

'Yes, and he's chosen some close-ups himself, I believe. Remember there's a time limit, though!' Audrey mimed a head being cut off.

'Where is he?' Maggie asked. But Audrey was already moving away.

Maggie looked around. At some invisible signal the congregation were starting to break from small chattering groups and settling into their seats. She sat down at the end of a row next to the aisle, clutching her list of questions. A hush gathered as most of the assembly looked reverentially forwards. Audrey settled the Minister in a prime position and then sat down next to him in the front row.

Maggie continued to search the hall, surprised by how many people she recognised. Debbie was on the other side of the aisle, gaudy and orange-tanned but carefully groomed; her husband next to her, swarthy and surly-looking. Sally, Maggie's landlady, was there with her two boys. There were a couple of people she recognised from the shop tills, and a short, stocky blonde woman she couldn't quite place in red trousers and a floral blouse.

She waved across at Graham, who was slumped with arms folded next to some of his ranger colleagues a few rows back, already looking bored. She supposed their work with the school must oblige them to be present. Finally, further back than Graham, she saw Trothan, his face mostly obscured by hair, sitting next to Nora who had her hands in her lap, smiling straight ahead. It was a relief to find they were here. Maggie knew they were back at home because she'd caught sight of Nora lumbering away from the shop towards her house earlier that day. The glimpse had also been welcome. Maggie wished she had the guts to sit down next to Trothan, to show herself connected to him.

Audrey stood up at the front on a level with her congregation, strolling from one side of the front row to the other as she spoke some words of welcome. She said tonight was their chance to celebrate some of the achievements of the school year, both personal and shared. She explained it was about diversity, not competition; that a few children's names had been pulled from a hat to present their favourite piece of work for the year.

'Pulled from a hat' was emphasised. Maggie guessed this was an attempt to quell the rage of parents whose children hadn't been picked, and to emphasise the fairness of the process.

Proceedings began. Children came up to the front to read from prepared scripts, their words a breathless torrent. A group of Primary Ones sang a song; a Primary Two girl talked about the hamster they had jointly looked after while Mrs Burt projected photos onto a big screen of the creature being carried to various homes for weekends and holidays by proud children. People clapped mechanically, glassy-eyed, but each performance was also greeted with smiles, camera flashes, even whoops of applause from one fragment of the audience.

Maggie's skin felt sticky in the heat of the hall, her nose and arm flaming with one-sided sunburn. She should have brought a bottle of water. She looked around, caught sight of another familiar figure: a man, tall and dark, with a boy of about twelve next to him who had a similarly long head and body. She suddenly realised it was PC Small, and then the short blonde woman who should have been beside him fell into place. Anderson in her red trousers. Of course, Maggie realised, each of them belonged to the community, each had their own family lives. She supposed herself an oddity being here without a child at the school. If she'd been a man, this would have provoked discomfort, perhaps even direct hostility.

Maggie noticed the damp dripping down the outside of the windows, a reminder of the grey wall of fog surrounding them; haar mingling with laundry steam. Midsummer fever lived on within the room in sunburnt faces, bared skin; the pre-holiday simmer of the whole community. She saw a gull swoop past the window. It made her feel as though the school was adrift, soaring and wheeling above its earthly footprint like the birds.

Then Trothan was on his feet in the aisle, swinging his wellies towards the front. The long map tube swung by his side almost weightily. The sight of his grin and a dark round eye peeking at her as he passed raised her from her seat to stride after him.

They both took a place beside Audrey at the front.

'Now,' Audrey said. 'The children from Primary Five have been doing their local studies projects and making maps. Trothan Gilbertson has also been developing his skills in his own time.'

A muffled cough came from the direction of Debbie's husband.

'He's going to put his map of the bay on the wall so you can go and have a close look afterwards.'

Trothan nodded away his fringe and smiled.

'But first. Maggie Thame, our local cartographer who's been helping him, will interview Trothan. We're in your hands then,' she said, turning and taking her seat next to the Minister.

The audience was silent.

Trothan was slowly unstoppering the cardboard tube. After pulling out a long roll of paper, he peered back inside and then closed it again, leaning it against the laptop console. Then he raised his arms, stretching the map between them in front of his face.

'Good evening everybody,' Maggie said to the mass of faces. She imagined how Carol would react if she could see her sister standing confidently in front of a crowd, nerves evaporated by pride. As if with a drum-roll she announced: 'So this is Trothan's map.'

She looked sideways, seeing the final map for the first time. Although the paper was intricately marked, the bold curve of the bay remained clearly defined. Trothan continued to hold it up, almost hiding, as the audience began to titter at the oddness of the spectacle. Maggie turned to Mrs Burt, and at a nod she projected the first slide behind their heads.

'You can put it down now,' Maggie whispered to Trothan. 'It's on the screen.'

Trothan dropped the paper map theatrically to his waist, revealing his grinning face. He rolled it up slowly. Maggie saw that the audience were all now looking behind them at the screen and glanced back herself, struck again by how the drawing and writing formed an intricate lace across it, even across the water of the bay itself.

She smiled some reassurance at Trothan and then asked the first question, partly in Trothan's direction and partly to the back row of seats, projecting her voice as she'd once been taught on a presentation skills course. 'Trothan, how long has this marvellous map taken you?'

He shrugged. 'Since you visited us, I suppose.'

'April. That's very quick. Can you tell us about your methods. What were your main tools?'

In the front row Audrey smiled and nodded encouragement. Getting to the script at last.

But Trothan became theatrical again. He pointed down at his legs, pulled a pencil out of his pocket, gestured at his eyes. 'And paper,' he said.

A titter scuttled about the audience.

'Did you draw the map straight off?'

'I did lots of sketches from different places.'

She drew from him where the places were and how he got to them. She expected him to explain how he'd built the drawings up in layers and finally made this composite. But when she glanced behind at the screen, she began to think he'd abandoned the composite approach, and simply started again, jamming together all his observations of whatever type into one enormous sketch-map. She could see the front elevations of buildings like the church, and how the shapes of copses, hills, cliffs were suggested pictorially.

She'd already spotted the submerged Spitfire in the bay, and St Coombs church under the sand dunes, and asked, as an aside to the scripted questions: 'So was it just what you could see that interested you?'

This question allowed him to point out some of the hidden features of the landscape that he'd made explicit. Each time she looked back, she became aware of more she hadn't seen in his drawings before and words she had no time to read. She would look properly later. The map simply looked a gorgeous thing. Highly detailed, figurative, but also conveying a real sense of geography, not only of the land, but the seabed, and the connections between them. She'd never seen anything quite like it. It seemed to take the artistic merit of early maps and the later passion for accurate geography, but then to add a further layer of story and subjective interpretation of the landscape. The seals and guillemots had been depicted in their own abstracted square of sea, which was seen from a sort of Picasso-esque perspective. That the creatures were 'flying' underwater was made clear by water-slicked fur and feather, and by the bubbles that rose from them.

Trothan gestured at Mrs Burt who went on to the next slide. The audience, looking over Maggie's shoulder, had the advantage of foreknowledge. She saw that one or two people tipped towards each other and whispered. The Minister leaned forward in polite scrutiny towards the screen, then turned briefly to Audrey, opened his eyes wide and looked back. The audience became like the sea's surface animated from beneath by a shoal of flickering fish.

She turned to the map to see what was causing it. At the top of Dunnet's church tower swung the huge bell, and it was being rung from below by a group of shackled black slaves. He had clearly drawn this from their brief conversation about the Oswalds. Her surprise at seeing this snippet of history revealed in a way which showed his distaste almost made her laugh out loud.

But now she remembered the audience and sought something else to comment on.

Near the harbour he'd drawn a circular building in stone, marked: 'ice house, now fish store.' She asked Trothan to talk about it.

'That's where they used to store the ice for the big house.' He pumped a finger towards the impression left by the burnt-down house surrounded by woodland.

'And it's a fish store now?' she asked, surprised to hear the murmur that this sent running through the hall.

Trothan nodded. 'And that's the boat that brings the fish.' He pointed at a drawing of a boat in the harbour. On its side the digits of its Scrabster port registration were clearly visible.

The audience murmured.

'It's fish they're not supposed to catch,' Trothan continued. 'Then someone takes it to people's houses to sell. And the hotels.'

The murmur rose again and reverberated around the hall. It was a collision of hilarity and embarrassment, she realised. Maggie had heard of 'black landings' of fish, and now she noticed weasel-faced Jim, arms folded, flushed but impassive, a few rows from the front. The congregation seemed complicit. Some of them would be customers themselves, she supposed, like herself. She saw Graham clap a hand across his eyes in mock-horror. She deliberately avoided looking at Audrey, who she imagined was clock-watching.

Trothan's grin was cracking his face now, and she decided to move things on. She pointed to a well on the shore near Murkle and asked about that.

'It was a holy well but the farmer dug up the special trough, so you can't see it any more,' he said.

A small disturbance turned heads. It was centred on a man with a red face and the woman beside him. They rattled against each other as if disturbed by a sudden gust.

She began to see what Trothan was doing; perhaps what the eighth layer of his map had been about. It made her think of surveillance: Burghley's use of a map to pinpoint Catholic-leaning households so they could be watched by the Elizabethan court; the Metropolitan Police reputedly tracking suspects and representing their movements as 3D graphics.

Audrey, sitting close to Maggie, caught her eye and held up two fingers; two minutes left.

'Would anyone else like to ask Trothan a question about his map?' She hoped this would broaden the discussion out again, return it to safer ground.

A hand went up a few rows back. One of the more boisterous pink girls she recognised from Trothan's class asked, 'Why are all the new bungalows built of bones?'

A babble of voices erupted from the audience and a gull-laugh flew out of Trothan. Pretty well pushing Mrs Burt out of the way, he went to the laptop and with a flick of the mouse, he zoomed in on one of the constructions. Sure enough, rather than breeze blocks, the fabric of the building was constructed from interlocking human bones. The drawing reminded Maggie of the image she'd had in her mind ever since Trothan talked about the loom weighted with human skulls.

Trothan started speaking without her prompt. 'That's because they're using sand from the dunes, and it has a very old graveyard in it. Vikings are buried there. Those are their bones.'

Maggie saw Graham stretch to upright in his seat. He turned to the person next to him, and said loudly enough that she could hear, 'Well, that explains a thing or two.'

She asked, for herself now, rather than on behalf of the audience. 'Who's digging the sand?'

Maggie saw that Trothan had positioned the cursor to highlight a new area of the map – the old church. He'd drawn it in elevation, showing its enormous door wide open. A truck was outside it unloading some substance that formed into mounds: sand.

There was a sudden scraping of chairs and Rab McNicholl was on his feet, pulling Debbie behind him; a bemused-looking daughter trailing them both. Graham turned to watch them go as the door slammed, muffling the curses.

Audrey made a cut-throat gesture at Maggie.

Maggie saw that Trothan was zooming in now on the pile of sand just inside the church door, the lines of his drawing getting ragged and blurred with magnification. Something long and slim was partially covered by the sand. Now they'd got the idea, people strained forward in their seats to see the detail of the drawing, a hum of speculation rising.

Maggie heard the Minister appeal to Audrey. 'Good grief, is that a...' Then Audrey was looming towards Maggie and Trothan, her forehead carved with a frown. Trothan left the laptop and picked up the cardboard tube, still apparently heavy. Maggie raised a hand to tell him that their time was up, but with one eye on the audience he pushed his hand inside the tube, and began gradually drawing something out. She dropped her hand

and watched as a chunky wooden butt appeared, followed by a tubular mounted eyesight and finally, slowly, a long black barrel. Instinctively she stepped back. He dropped the cardboard tube, and brandished the gun high in the air above his head, grinning broadly, reminding her of a terrifying Milky-Bar Kid.

Chairs scraped. Trothan brought the eyepiece to his face and was pointing the long dark barrel directly at weasel-faced Jim.

Most people were stunned into stillness, but Audrey strode up to Trothan, slapped his arm down and grappled the gun from him. Chairs tumbled as PC Small burst forward to fell Trothan with a lunge to his legs. Chaos followed. Maggie, separated from Trothan by these scuffles, just had time to see that he was still grinning through a flurry of hair and tumbling limbs. Even through the sound of furniture crashing, and the clamour of adult voices and girlish shrieks, she heard him laughing. Nora was on her feet and grim at the back, the broad shape of a man, a father perhaps, next to her.

People were ushered out, calm gradually returning, chairs stacked by parent-helpers.

'Want a lift home, Maggie?' Graham was at her side.

She tried to shrug him off, keen to see the evening to its conclusion. Audrey and PC Small were leading Trothan and his parents into a corner, and she wanted to hear what was said.

'Let's go,' Graham insisted, taking her arm.

'Little devil,' she heard from one of the departing parents behind her.

'We won't be expecting him back for the remaining days of the term,' Audrey said to Nora before spinning on her heel away from the huddle around Trothan to oversee the return of order to the hall.

Maggie just had time to see, before she was steered out, that

Trothan's head was bent now, a shiver in his shoulders suggesting tears, and she felt it as a blow fisted into her own guts. The undisplayed map dangled limply from his hand.

FIFTEEN

She woke the next morning with a sense that someone else was in the house. Sunlight was seeping through the thin lining of the curtains and at midsummer that could mean anything later than three a.m. She looked at her watch and saw that it was six. Had she locked the door when she came in the night before? She couldn't be sure, her habits had become so muddled. She lay still, listening, but there was nothing more than that initial sense of intrusion.

She eased herself from the edge of the bed, imagining what Carol would say: 'Why didn't you just phone 999? Surely you keep the phone by the bed?' Next, she'd be suggesting a gun. Then the events of the previous night came rushing back.

Despite the idiocy of Carol's fears, Maggie was aware of her heart cantering, obscuring the sounds that might be beyond her bedroom door. Making a quick search of the room, she grabbed the bulky hardback, Blaeu's *Atlas Maior*, the only thing of any weight in the room. Holding it ahead of her, she left the bedroom, bare feet whispering down the corridor towards the glass sitting room door.

As she approached, a small figure in a bright blue sweatshirt became visible. He'd chosen her. He'd come to her in what she assumed to be his trauma from the previous night. She could see him standing completely still and facing the chair on which the sealskin hung, his kelp-wild hair strung over his shoulders. By edging a little to the side, she saw through the glass that both his hands rested on the pelt so he almost seemed in communion with it.

She let the Atlas hang down and opened the door quietly, coming to stand beside Trothan without either of them turning to look at the other.

'So,' she said quietly, towards his hands. 'You've met my visitor.' There was something rumpled and salty about both.

He murmured a word or two that she didn't catch.

'God knows where it came from. I found it in my loft.'

Trothan's face was still down-turned but she could see trouble there, a resemblance to the pale boy at school who stayed up all night with his games. The almond-shaped eyes squinting slightly, red-rimmed. His sweatshirt smeared with green; hair rough; face sand-speckled. *Child,* she enunciated to herself, longing to reach out and give him a hug.

'Trothan,' she said, remembering his hilarity as he grappled with the gun. 'You gave a lot of people a fright last night. You do realise that?'

He carried on looking straight ahead.

'Where did it come from? What were you doing with it?' she asked, knowing that this wouldn't help, but despite herself. 'You didn't really mean to…?'

The long cardboard tube lay across the table.

'Have you been carrying that around all night?' she asked gently.

He looked at her then, eyes piercing the fringe, his hand staying on the skin, stroking to and fro down the centre of what had been the seal's face.

'You've not been expelled, have you?' She pictured him imprisoned somewhere in a boarding school instead of his life off the leash here. She realised she must stop asking him questions. Let him be, she told herself. Let him be.

'I'll make some hot chocolate. Have a lie down on the sofa if you like.'

When she returned, the child had drawn the seal pelt around his shoulders as if it was a coat. The low morning light through the window silvered it, creating an animal litheness out of the union. She gathered the tail of the pelt that trailed the floor behind him and tucked it under Trothan's arm. He grinned down at it. Then he looked up at her, pursed his lips and nodded. He started to walk almost trance-like towards the door as if she had given him permission.

'Trothan,' she called after him.

His hand was on the door handle.

'Have your hot chocolate first.'

He was opening the door.

'Do your parents know where you are?'

He paused with the door open and half turned back. She felt an urgency to detain him, the same tight panic as when he disappeared in Rab McNicholl's church; that clouded face seen through thick green water. Trothan and yet not Trothan.

'And don't forget your map,' she picked the tube up from the table. But he was already out of the door. She saw his face, its odd flat profile, pass first one window, then the next. Something stopped her from following him, some recognition of a private intent that she couldn't understand. He glided past the third window, drawn by something. Where was he going? Home, she hoped. His parents would be able to deal with this; should know him well enough. She didn't have enough experience with children.

But a minute or so later she saw a couple of flashes amongst the trees below her garden. Like the deer she saw running through there, the shimmer of silky light between trunks suggested speed; he must be heading for the sea.

She considered phoning his parents but it was still so early. On the dot of seven, she dialled. The mother's groggy morning voice eventually responded.

'Nora,' Maggie said. 'It's Maggie. The map woman.' She couldn't bring herself to use the word 'lady' as everyone else did.

'Yes?' An edge of anxiety.

'It's Trothan.'

'About last night?' Nora huffed.

'He's been here.'

Silence.

'This morning,' Maggie said.

There were a series of mutters. She heard the mother say: 'Is he not in his room?' Presumably to the father.

Nora's voice came back, urgent, penetrating: 'Where is he now?'

'I don't know. I couldn't stop him.' Pathetic. She was pathetic. But how did his parents have so little control over him? 'It looked like he hadn't slept.'

A tussle with the phone; clunks.

Now the father's voice, rough and direct. 'When did he leave?'

She looked at her watch. 'Thirty minutes ago.' Guilt beginning its tug.

'Thanks for letting us know.' A dialling tone. When she tried to call back there was no answer.

Her trouser legs were wet with dew when she reached the tussocks at the back of the dunes half an hour later. Through the nick between them she saw a 'V' of sea and a spray-wet beach appearing, waves rearing. The wind was strong. She descended, wading up to her shins in the sand's cold depths. On one quick glance up, she thought she saw a misted figure on the flat of sand out towards Dunnet. The figure reorganised everything around it visually, all the horizontals. When she looked up again, it had disappeared amidst the spray. Damn, she thought, could that have been him?

She reached the beach, paused and gazed in both directions. She was on the no-man's-land between the two villages, two promontories. She walked towards Dunnet. The wave-pulse and her rhythmic footsteps began to beat a calm back into her; her breath steadying her heart. Trothan would probably be at home now, getting cleaned up; eating breakfast. Although, she recalled, he would not be going off to school as usual.

Her feet stayed on the landward side of the shoreline frill, leading her on a meandering path. Two dark round heads bobbed up, rolling with the swell. When they turned their heads, she saw that they had the long, wise noses of the grey seals that came to these waters, not the smaller common seals. They stayed alongside her, visible every now and again as they rose and fell beyond the surf.

Once again, a long way away, near to the rocks at Dunnet but partly obscured in spray, she thought she saw another human figure. Then gone. She continued to walk, watching her feet, so that when she looked up and saw the man, a little shock fizzed through her.

Maggie prepared her face, smiling up at him as if from a reverie when they were a few feet from each other, and was confused by his manner, focussed almost rudely on her.

'Good morning,' she called out, making a defence of good manners.

His steps slowed, and so did hers, as if this was an intentional meeting. He was a shortish, wide man, and faintly familiar. His eyes were blue and the skin around them was folded and wrinkled with laugh lines. Not that he was laughing now.

'Lovely morning,' she said to cover her embarrassment.

'A midsummer walk?' He looked at her and shuffled slightly. His face was weighted into fleshy folds.

'I thought I was alone,' she said.

He hesitated a moment before breaking the awkwardness. 'We know each other, already, in a way,' he said.

Had she met him in the pub, forgotten him in her whisky haze?

'I'm Trothan's Dad.'

'Is he back home?' she demanded, politeness forgotten.

He looked vaguely over the top of her head, jowly and serious. He could have been taken for the boy's grandfather. But then, Maggie thought, he matched the mother, in the sense of his age and having no visible resemblance to Trothan. She wondered from where the boy got his petite beauty.

'You're not looking for him, are you?' he asked.

'I was hoping he was on his way home when he left my house.'

The father seemed to survey the beach himself now. He passed a hand over his face.

'But you're looking for him?' she asked.

The father looked out to sea and scanned the horizon as if

he hadn't heard her. 'Likely we'll not be seeing the lad today,' he said.

'Oh?'

The father raised a hand in a small wave and turned, legs tick-tocking him away from her. He occasionally looked out to sea or back in her direction. But mostly he stared straight ahead, apparently striking out towards his breakfast. He didn't look like a man with a missing son.

She stood still on the sand watching him diminish and eventually disappear from sight. With nothing else to do, she turned for home.

SIXTEEN

The phone rang as soon as she got in. She rushed at it, her high intonation demanding something. 'Yes?'

'Richard here,' the voice said. 'You okay?'

'Yes.'

'Sure?'

'Yes.'

'Well,' he said. 'I was just phoning to check we're still on course for the end of the day.'

'Yes,' she said mechanically. 'The proof pages will be with you by five o'clock. They're not ready yet, but they will be.' It seemed irrelevant now but efficiency was a habit.

'Great. I'll get back to you with the edits within a week, then you've still got a week before you submit. You've got enough time today?'

'I've got the whole day.' She seemed to be reassuring herself that it was still possible to turn things around within it.

'The longest day,' he said. 'And a lovely one.'

'Lovely?'

'Lovely here,' he said, 'is it raining there?'

'No,' she said. 'It's sunny. Hot day. Wild sea.'

'Odd,' he said.

After she put the phone down she turned on the computer, stared at its illuminating face for a while, made a few notes. But it wasn't long before she was standing at the window, wondering.

She set out on her bicycle not really knowing where she was going. She just had to be looking. She kept reminding herself that he could just be hiding; lying low. She repeated it to herself like a mantra. Across the fields, inland, were numerous wartime look-outs and bunkers, underground hide-outs into which a boy could disappear. But there were also many hazards. Images jostled in her head: Trothan lying as still as the rubble below him after falling through a roof or floating face down in the harbour.

Her own memories were simultaneously raised to swing on a gantry, slicked grey with salt-mud, like the debris in tidal rivers near towns. Supermarket trolleys, discarded dolls, bicycle wheels dredged up so their lines clarified as they dripped.

She remembered how once, as a child, she'd felt excluded by Carol and her friends who'd come to play. Maggie had climbed into the coal bunker and earthed herself into its darkest corner, waiting for the family to notice her absence. She finally started to hear her name being called, footsteps passing. Utterly miserable, coal-dusted and tear-smeared, she'd emerged voluntarily, expecting a rapturous welcome, only to be shouted at by her mother, and have her face roughly scrubbed with a flannel. She was then sent to her room.

She understood the reaction better now and recalled how an hour or so later her mother had come in with a glass of warm milk and a chocolate biscuit.

When she reached the harbour, she left her bike and took the path through the old flagstone works, wandering between stone linings and walls which surfaced craggily through grass; relics from a prosperous past. The whole place was on the creep. There were concealed shafts and tunnels and signs warning you to stick to the paths. Three cats were skulking, round-backed, on top of a wall. Sinister and thuggish even in broad daylight, they guarded their territory as if gatekeepers of some kind of underworld.

'Where is he?' She wanted to say to them. 'And where's everyone else?' It was well after nine now, when the morning should have been in full swing, and yet everywhere seemed deserted.

But at the harbour Mobility Man was parked up – a fluorescent flare next to the bench where she and Carol had met him before. He sat gripping the scooter's handlebars, cigarette dangling at the corner of his mouth. When she approached, he gestured at her to sit down.

She shook her head, the wind batting at her bicycle as she held it up. 'I'm looking for someone.'

He nodded.

'A boy,' she added.

His nod this time was barely discernible.

'You haven't seen him, have you?'

A slight jerk in his neck indicated a question.

'Trothan,' she said. 'Trothan Gilbertson. You haven't seen him, have you?'

He shook his head quite clearly now. She got back on her bicycle.

'It's that time of year,' he said just as she was about to push off. His hands came off the handlebars and parted wide, as if demonstrating expansion.

'Sorry?'

He nodded towards the heaving sea, then looked up towards

the sky. 'All that light,' he said slowly.

She thought perhaps he was right, that any child would avoid school on such a day as this. But perhaps he hadn't heard yet what had happened last night. Trothan was in disgrace, excluded from school for pointing a gun at the fisherman who might be Mobility Man's son.

The waves near them were sucked back and thrown forward; a rhythmic breathing, catching in their motion a dancing light. She saw the flashes of something feral again between foliage, careering in this direction.

'He looked like he hadn't slept,' she said.

He shook his head. 'He'll not be a good sleeper. Those that the tides wash through, eh?'

'Sorry?'

'It's not restful.'

Mobility Man's wrists rested on the bars, still wide. And then as she gathered herself again for departure, he let them fall away from each other, allowing the contained world he'd created between them to collapse. He seemed even more mad than the last time she'd met him.

Back at the cottage her work lay waiting for her; a message on the phone was signalled by a red flashing light. Richard. She ignored it.

She picked up the phone and dialled. The voice that answered lilted with anxiety.

'Nora?'

'Yes?'

She didn't know what to say, and a silence hung awkwardly for a moment. 'It's Maggie. I met your husband on the beach this morning.'

There was a pause, then, 'Yes, he told me.' Her voice gave nothing away.

'I wondered from what he said if Trothan was not exactly missing, but...'

Breathing on the line.

'I just wondered.'

'How can I help you?' The mother's voice was level compared to her own.

'I just wondered if he'd turned up.'

Silence again. 'Don't worry about it, please.'

'I was just concerned.' And then she added into the silence, 'as a friend.'

'There's no need.'

Relief began to flood in. 'He's back, then?'

She heard muffled voices as though the mother had turned from the phone, her hand over it while a discussion took place. There were some scuffling noises and then a man's brisk voice, the softness of this morning grazed off. 'There's no need for you to bother.'

Impatience was rising in her now. 'Is he still missing?'

'He's not missing.'

'Well, do you know where he is?' She sounded like Carol.

Silence.

'Hello?'

'It's nothing you need get involved in, this.'

'Well, surely it's time to involve the police?' she said.

'We've just said goodbye to them,' he said. And then there was a click at the other end. The dialling tone again. Maggie slammed the phone down.

Charged up with strong coffee, she sat down to work. She

opened all the relevant files and made a list of tasks.

Ignoring the unresolved problem of Lagos's expansion, she decided to start with a small map representing the flow of cocoa exports between countries. It was similar to one she'd already done to show the dispersal of slaves from West Africa during the Atlantic Slave Trade. Arrows swept across the oceans like irrepressible currents and drifts. But cocoa involved the whole world, and the density of the arrows needed to represent statistics.

She imported a world map file and started to fill the polygons for each country with the relevant colours, orange for 'Main Consumers' and green for 'Main Producers', which made a stark division between northern and southern regions of the map. Then she started to pay attention to the statistical charts which Richard had provided, sitting with the calculator in one hand and her head in the other.

A car settled on the gravel outside; the engine cut. She leapt up. Anderson and Small were getting out of a police car, holding on to their hats.

'Is there are any news? Have you found him?' Maggie looked from face to face as they reached the open door.

'May we come in? It would be helpful if we could take a statement from you,' Small said.

'Of course.'

Anderson sat down on the sofa, ready to take notes; Small on the armchair with the questions. 'We're obviously very concerned about the gun and where it came from.'

'Not about the boy?' she blurted.

'We assume that you helped Trothan Gilbertson with the incriminating information he put on the map.'

'Most of it was as much of as a surprise to me as anyone.'

'Come now,' said Anderson. 'Why did that child have a gun?'

'What?' She felt the blood flash up to her face.

'I think you must've known a little of what he was up to. You got him making the map by all accounts.'

'Whose accounts?'

'They all credit you,' Small said. 'The headteacher, even the boy's parents.'

She felt a weary, downward pull. 'It wasn't loaded, was it? The gun.'

She saw Small's hands tighten around one knee. 'No, the gun wasn't loaded, thank goodness, or we might have had a major tragedy on our hands. Now. His mother tells us the lad had a hide-out of some sort in the old farm buildings here.' He indicated over his shoulder.

'Did he?' Maggie asked.

Small looked at her and bit his lip, apparently irritated.

'I've seen a collection of things in there,' she said. 'Bones, shells, things from the beach. But I didn't know it had anything to do with Trothan.' A glimmer of possibility stood her upright. 'So maybe that's where...'

Small gestured at her seat. 'It's already been checked.'

She sat down again.

'What took you in there, then?' Small asked.

Why did she explore anywhere? 'I'm naturally inquisitive, I suppose.'

'Intrusive?' Anderson looked up from her note-taking as if about to make an amendment.

Maggie enunciated each syllable: '"Inquisitive", I said.'

Small breathed deeply, as if allowing this insolence. 'And when was it you took him to the old church?'

'He took me!' she said.

Small stared at her. 'Which one of you was the child?'

She let this beat through her. He was right. 'It was about ten days ago,' she said.

'And did you go inside on that occasion?'

'No.'

'But the lad did?'

'Yes.'

'Did he seem to know it, to have been there before?'

'Yes.'

'Did you go back? Together? Separately?'

'Not that I know of.'

'Any indication that he found anything there when you went with him?'

'He came out holding a bone. At the time I thought it couldn't be a bone. It looked a bit like a finger bone. But perhaps it was, after all, from the Viking burial. Is that where they were storing the sand from the beach?'

Small ignored her question. 'No sign of a gun?'

'That's where he found it?'

'Might he have carried it out? In a coat or a bag?'

She shook her head, noticing in this light that Small's eyes were blue, very clear, very sharp. He was enjoying his power.

'How do you know it came from there?' she asked.

'Let's say Rab McNicholl owed us a favour.'

'It was his?'

'Best not to speculate. Likely he was letting someone else use the place for their tools or whatever.'

'Shouldn't you be out pursuing them?'

Small edged forward in his seat, lips pale. 'We have our procedures.' He glanced at Anderson. 'That will be all for now. PC Anderson will just write up your statement for you to sign.'

Maggie looked over at Anderson's head bent like a primary pupil with a biro plodding across a jotter.

'Please don't go anywhere without telling us,' Small said.

Maggie found herself on her feet, but sat down again quickly. 'So what about the boy, the missing child?'

A glance shuffled between the two officers.

'Mrs Thame,' the tall man said. 'When you've lived and worked here as long as we have. Well,' he paused. 'The boy's whereabouts isn't police business at the moment. We don't get involved unless necessary in domestic matters.'

She stared at the man. 'But his own father doesn't know where he is.'

'Noone has reported a missing person. Not at this stage,' Small said.

'But he's not at home?'

Small pursed his lips.

'And he's not here,' she said.

'As you know he likes to wander. And I think the parents know what to expect, and when things are out of the ordinary. Naturally we intend to interview him just as soon as...'

'So where is it you think he is?' Maggie interrupted.

'Forgive me, Mrs Thame, but I understand you don't have children yourself?'

She flopped back in her chair, defeated.

'There are different styles of parenting. We have to respect that as police. They believe, and so do we, that the lad will turn up once he's licked his wounds. He's an independent sort. And this is a rural area, not Oxford.'

A little electric shock connected her to her past. Swallowing her hurts, she asked: 'What happens now?'

'As I said, please don't leave without telling us,' he said.

'The house? The country?' she asked.

The phone rang at about four.

'How's it going, Maggie?'

'Getting there.'

'I'll be leaving the office in just under an hour, right?'

'I know,' she snapped. Why did he phone her? She'd never missed a deadline in her life. 'Sorry, Richard. Too much caffeine.'

'Yes,' he said. 'I can hear it bubbling.'

'Can you bear with me on the Lagos population graphic? I need to think about it a bit more.'

'Sure,' he said.

She simply couldn't raise enough creative concentration for it at the moment. She sent everything else off to him at one minute to five and sat back, relieved to have finished but now aware of opening a door for something else to prowl through.

Carol phoned.

'What children need is constant supervision from a caring and responsible parent,' she lectured.

Carol had asked so many questions that Maggie had eventually admitted that Trothan seemed to have gone into hiding.

'Do you think they'll take him away?' Carol asked.

'Who?'

'The authorities. Take Trothan from his parents. If he comes back, I mean,' Carol added.

Maggie was stunned into a few seconds' silence. 'Is that likely?'

'Well, they haven't even reported him missing?'

'No.' But Maggie had to admit to herself now that she didn't even know if he was missing.

'If they're not parenting him properly, letting him wander to unsuitable places. Hang around unsuitable people.'

Maggie thought for a moment. 'Are you talking about me?'

After putting the phone down, she googled: 'Boy missing, Quarrytown', but nothing came up, except the story that Trothan had told her about Peter Barker disappearing with a woman in green.

Evening wouldn't come. It was the longest Longest Day she had ever known. When she raised her head, the first thing she registered was Trothan's usual seat at the table – empty. The absence took a strange, dark, rounded shape. She wondered if being a parent felt like this; even when your child was away from you, their presence so visceral it could raise the hair on your arms?

Perhaps Lizzy Ginner lived on for her parents through the shadow of what she might have become. A gymnast perhaps, or an assiduous reader of Harry Potter books. An ear to the door of her empty bedroom might betray the breathing of a radiator as if she were still sleeping there. In the sea on holidays her memory would swim close to her parents; a bump against a hip, the wash of displaced water.

Maggie recalled how after the accident a woman had run out of her front door and then gone back in again, returning with a high visibility fluorescent coat, a huge one. They'd wrapped the tiny child in it as she lay on the mother's lap.

In her daydreams, Maggie's car wouldn't start that day. She'd have walked to work or caught the bus, drifting sleepily past Oxford's spires and Pakistani shops. Another daydream had her as the hero, two cars behind the accident. She'd run forward, be kneeling within the tight circle of helpers with the mother. Her quick thinking in bringing the wool rug from the car would help maintain the child's life till the ambulance came; quite possibly save her. In her daydreams she wasn't the one standing apart with urine-soaked trousers, watching helplessly.

Lit up by evening sun beaming through her sitting room window, she sat with her head in her hands. The only one apparently concerned about Trothan's whereabouts, she had to act, search, call his name, protect him. But how? Then Maggie suddenly remembered the archaic script on the OS Map that identified a churchyard at the foot of Olrig Hill.

Trees threw long crisp shadows across the lush grass; trees that enclosed and sheltered Saint Trothan's graveyard. It was as if she'd stepped into a different day, still and hazy with hovering insects, the sharp tap-tapping of stonechats. High above her the swishing of foliage recalled the blustery evening continuing beyond the walls.

With hope spreading its wings, she was drawn towards the shade at the back of the graveyard where the dampest, deepest grass grew, beyond the enclosures of iron railings decoratively wrought, once in manufacture and then again by tangled ivy. Climbing steps up onto a low stone platform towards the church, supine gravestones offered themselves like great paving slabs, some moss-covered, some hinting at an engraved letter or number. The place seemed miniature in scale compared to everything else in Caithness with its expanses of flat, wet moorland. It was like some jewelled enclave of Cornwall, where you could reach out and touch stone and moss, and the land closed tightly around you.

The slabs led her to a series of closely-packed, upright gravestones carved with skulls and crossbones and names like Donald Swanson, Elizabeth Manson, Sinclair Waters, and even some Gilbertsons. One stone in the shadiest, dankest spot near the back wall stopped her; a flat stone with a deep hollow in it and no inscription. It was filled with greenish water. The sight made her catch her breath.

Once through the low doorway of the church, she looked up to see huge branches criss-crossing the sky where the roof had been. Trothan flickered there briefly, perched high up with his hair swinging, laughing at her. Then gone. It was a curious thing that she found herself equally able to picture him as an angel or a gargoyle.

She stood in the open church listening. There was a sense of murmuring, and it was hard to say whether it came from the birds or the sigh of foliage or from the old stone walls themselves. Ancient bells echoing far off, booming through watery curtains.

She went outside again. The surface of the pool in the stone gave off a silvery reflection, but she could see down to where tendrils of its mossy lining washed slightly as if in a current. Since she'd been in the church, some greenery had blown in and now floated at its centre like seaweed. She looked around, almost expecting an impish face to twitch back behind a gravestone. It was as if Trothan was nearby, teasing her. But the stillness around her gave nothing away, however much she searched the shadows and willed the child to reveal himself by a stifled giggle or a shimmer of movement.

'Trothan?' she tried the name aloud and waited. Nothing.

She'd had no impulse to pray since childhood. Back then it had been after some irreversible wrongdoing when she asked God to put the clock back, to alter the route she'd taken or what she'd said. She was aware now of being in a place of deep echoes; of the year cracking open at the solstice with her perched in the abyss between its two halves. She might stray to a place that only existed at Midsummer and have to wait until the following solstice to be spat back up again, or perhaps wait another seven years.

With eyes closed in prayer by the strange green pool, Midsummer illusions – appearances, disappearances, half-human creatures, God even – all became real; all possible. She was sucked down, caught in the heart of a roller, tumbled and disorientated. But her eyes seemed to open into the green and white hurly-burly, into water thick with sand. And she glimpsed hair straggling like kelp and a tiny face plunging past her, mouth gaping and swallowing water, eyes pinched shut. A turmoil of lashing hair. And then it was gone, beyond the reach of her outstretched fingers.

By the time she cycled home, the north-west horizon had roared red and then lulled to purple and pink; the wind stilling with it. Overhead a strange translucence hung on. There were no longer any shadows.

Distant dogs complained from somewhere as she freewheeled down the lane. She had no lights but could see enough of her watch-face to know it was around midnight. Across the grey-lit sloping fields she could see the corrugated outline of the dunes, the sky still faintly luminous behind them. But between her and the dunes, a string of lights blinked. She pulled up at the gate of the cottage to watch. The way the lights swung and trembled showed that they were torches carried by hand.

She knew it was common at the two ends of the year in northern latitudes; burning ships, screaming youths leaping through fires, wild drinking. She'd even heard of an old rite in which cowherds walked the perimeter of their folds on Midsummer's eve with torches to purify and protect the land.

But did they really still do that here?

Then there was another light. A single one, much closer, moving amongst the derelict farm buildings not far below her. The light vanished and she heard slight creaking as if someone was walking across fallen masonry. Someone was in the barn.

Two late birds rose from the ragged silhouette of a ruined wall, their wing beats cleanly enunciated as they approached and flapped over her towards the village. Her own wings rose then, a flutter in her stomach. Trothan would be in his lair curling around his sea-treasures, seeking refuge in sleep: Trothan had come back.

SEVENTEEN

She left the bike and strode down to the end of the lane. A car was parked beside the gate, a bird-watcher perhaps. But as she climbed the gate and started across the field it was the barn that pulled her into a run, elation elbowing aside any thoughts about the car or the dancing of far torches.

Her footfall was hushed by the grass path leading into the farm courtyard. She paused. In this odd placid light, neither day nor night, the entrance to the barn was less obvious than she expected, the distances distorted. A breeze sighed in some loose iron sheeting as she located the dark gash of doorway and hurried towards it.

The interior of the barn was a gloomy cavity except where torchlight flared in the far corner. It made silhouettes of the strewn wreckage on the floor and threw the shadow of a gigantic figure onto the far wall, its back hunched over something. A rhythmic noise came from the corner. A gulping and puffing.

'Trothan?' she said. The noises all wrong. All ugly.

There was a gasp. A crackle of clothing as the silhouette turned sharply and Maggie realised her mistake, her inner flight crashing to the ground.

'Nora,' she said, aware that she couldn't be seen, at least not in any clear way. 'It's Maggie.'

She started to make her way over then, getting down to use her hands where she needed to, unable to see rusty nails, sharp edges. Just the clattering of loose boards in her ears and splinters in her hands and her heart thumping.

'Sorry to give you a fright,' she said as she reached Nora, who was kneeling on the blanket Trothan had presumably left there. She took a deep breath. 'I thought he'd come back. When I saw the torchlight.'

Nora lowered her wild head; shook it.

Maggie saw by the dim light of the torch, now lying in the folds of the blanket, the red cuffs of Nora's parka and that she held a large white pebble in one hand; a bone in the other. It was the bone Maggie had associated with the shape of a dolphin's fin. Graham had doubled over with laughter when she'd suggested this. It was a seabird's breast bone, he'd said, with a prominent sternum. She'd learnt that much since moving to this bird-dense end of the world.

'So this is his den?' Maggie said, kneeling down near Nora on the edge of the blanket, picking up a gull's feather.

Nora nodded.

'I didn't know about it,' Maggie said. 'Why here?'

Nora took a guttering breath and looked up so that the torchlight from below outlined some curls, sculpted her face with goblinish shadows. 'It's where he liked to go. When we lived here.'

A dark rift opened up in Maggie. 'When you lived here?'

Nora nodded, raised a hand towards Flotsam Cottage.

Maggie stared at her.

'He didn't tell you? We lived here, not for long. We had burst pipes, it was while the damage was mended.'

'When?'

'Just before you moved in.'

Maggie slumped down onto the blanket, re-organising everything in her mind. She thought of the child's ease in the place, the times he'd turned up at her door so soon after her arrival home in the afternoon as if he'd been nearby, watching. Feathers tangled in his hair. And yesterday morning – *this* morning – his slept-rough look when he'd appeared so early in her sitting room.

Nora looked at her hands curling upwards on each knee. She took a deep breath. 'We thought he'd be back by now too,' she said hoarsely.

'I can't understand,' Maggie tried to compose her voice. 'Why no one was bothered.'

She heard the crackle of Nora's abrupt movement again. 'What do you mean by that?'

'Why the police, you, didn't start looking.'

'No,' said Nora.

Maggie heard a sort of admission and wanted more.

'No,' Nora said again. 'You wouldn't understand.'

Maggie fought against a storm. Remained seated.

'It's not the first time he's annoyed people with his ways,' Nora said. 'But this time he's in trouble. Big trouble.' As she said the last two words the whites of her eyes glimmered through darkness. 'The police have been back and forth all day. Interviewing us. Wanting to talk to him.'

Maggie found herself trembling. Why had Nora started to care about her son now? 'I had no idea that there was a gun. I didn't even know about his den here. About the sand, or the

Viking bones, or the black fish.'

'Apparently it was you that got him going with that...' Nora seemed to struggle to articulate the words with enough disgust. 'That map thing.'

Maggie leapt up to standing, wobbling slightly on the uneven boards.

'Why did you want to show up everyone like that?' Nora demanded.

'I just encouraged his mapmaking. That involves going to places. But he went further, he must've been digging about.' It was true that Trothan's map seemed to have a moralistic element, a determination to expose people.

Nora looked up at her now through the gloom.

A still sea spread between the two women. They both seemed to wait. Maggie's breathing almost painfully loud, a twist in her gut. She sat back down, kept her head low.

'What happens now?' she asked quietly.

Nora gestured behind with her head. 'You'll have seen them. Mountain rescue, the dog unit coming, the whole lot of them.'

'A search?' Maggie realised now what the torches must have been. A sweep of searchers moving inland from the beach.

No answer came. There was no sense of movement.

When Nora did speak it was unexpected. 'So you saw him last?'

'As far as I know.'

Nora gathered her hands towards each other, breathed deeply again. 'Did he take anything? From the cottage.'

Maggie shook her head. 'He left his map.' And then she pictured him again as he'd been when he left, wrapped in the pelt, the way it fell around his shoulders transforming to a coat of mist. 'And I gave him a sealskin – he went off with it.'

Nora was rising up from the blanket onto her knees, awkward and unsteady, her shiny face looming towards Maggie. 'Why?'

'He just seemed to like it. He seemed sad.'

Nora was close to her, staring.

'I don't even know why it was in the cottage,' Maggie said, realising a possibility as she said it. 'Do you?'

After a moment Nora nodded.

'Why?'

Nora thrashed away from her with a gust of breath. 'It meant a lot to him when he was wee,' she said.

'So it was his anyway. Why shouldn't he have it, then? And why did you leave it here anyway?'

There was no immediate answer.

'Did you leave it?'

Maggie recalled the last time Nora had been here, collecting Trothan. It was after that she found the sealskin. Might Trothan have put it in the loft himself?

'Didn't you see the danger?' Nora's volume was rising, her voice beginning to yowl. 'He was fragile yesterday morning after all that carry-on.'

There was a gap. A gap in what had been said and understood. Maggie heard the blame and braced herself against it. All that great weight to heave around.

Nora's accusation trailed into a scoffing noise. She paused on an intake of breath, bosom inflated inside her red parka, then rose to her feet, turning to scrabble her way back across the chaotic floor, the torchlight pitching about the floor and walls as she made her seasick crossing. Finally the listing figure was silhouetted against the grey light of the entrance, one arm stretched out for balance.

Maggie, collecting herself too late, called after her, 'Do you have the car? Can I give you a lift home?'

But Nora had gone.

First swelling of morning light. The throb of a low-flying Sea King summoned her out of bed to a window. Cars stopping in the lane. Lots of them. Doors slamming; voices. Maggie looked out at accumulating cars with white, red and blue stripes; huddles of black uniforms, caps going on. Steps sounded on the gravel and a dark shape passed one window, then another. Finally PC Small was framed in the glass of the door, knuckles raised and about to strike when he saw her approaching.

He took his hat off. 'Morning,' he said. 'Mind if I come in?'

'So you're finally taking it seriously? The disappearance?'

'We'll need to take another statement from you. About when you last saw the lad.'

There was something she wasn't going to be allowed to know. She let him in. 'Coffee?'

'Please,' he said, preparing for the interview by laying out paper and pens at the table.

She glanced out of the window. Andersons and Smalls, cloned, had been released in long parallel marching lines alongside Gore-Tex-uniformed mountain rescuers, to scramble over the jagged masonry of the old farm buildings and beyond. She sensed the trajectories of other search parties she couldn't see. Over the coarse grass of the dunes, out past the brick World War II huts, through the shifting strata of the flagstone works. All the fishing boats on alert.

PC Anderson came in without knocking. Maggie's house seemed to have become public property. She made coffee, answered questions on what Trothan had been wearing, what he'd said, who she thought his friends were. They wanted to know all the places significant to the lad, and where he might have gone. She unrolled his map across the table and stood a mug on each corner to keep it flat. It made best sense to show them like this, even though it felt an act of betrayal.

'So he left this here,' Anderson indicated the map. 'He wasn't carrying anything else?'

Something made her hold back. She wasn't sure why. It was almost as if she was colluding with Nora.

They searched her house, wanted to know if he'd ever spent a night, which rooms he went to when he visited. As if she might be imprisoning him in a basement. How could such a spirit be imprisoned anyway? An Ariel in a tree trunk.

Then they were leaving.

'You don't think, do you?' A hectic flapping of alarm in her. 'He couldn't be in danger from anyone he incriminated?' She thought of the church and Rab McNicholl, his brute of a dog.

'We'll be doing all we can.' PC Anderson sounded almost sympathetic.

And they left, asking her again not to leave without letting them know.

Their car rumbled off towards missing person reports, interviews, incident rooms, press releases. Left her to silence.

She wanted him back in this room. She longed to hear his mischievous laugh or to see him balancing on the log over the burn. She wanted him safe and by her side with their rituals resumed.

Instead she kept seeing an image of a child with its eyes and chin raised towards something; a strange enchantment drawing it into danger.

Two days later Trothan had still not returned. Her feet took her. Pounding down to the harbour; past the harbour and onto the beach. If she could walk along a steady undemanding surface she would be soothed. Walk and walk and walk. To Dunnet and back. Two hours. Two hours which she wouldn't need to fill with anything else; when she would need nothing to distract her.

The tide was out. The sand a great shining apron from the base of the dunes. Near the Dunnet end a few people with dogs had spilled onto the beach from the caravan site. But, there. A single figure standing ahead; a woman. Her arms were by her sides as she stood mid-beach and stared towards the horizon. She wore a red jacket. With a lurch, Maggie realised it was Nora. She beat away, heading towards the tower of Dunnet church, where cloud was stacked in blocks high above the village.

The perpendicular figure in this field of endless horizontals remained in Maggie's mind. Twice she looked back and saw that Nora was still there. A monument dividing the landscape.

At the far end of the bay, sand and water gave into rock that scrambled up to meet turf, grass, buildings. She wanted to stay longer at this meeting place of one slip against another. But finally she turned and started to walk back. An almost wintry wind hurt her head and it began to rain.

Nora was no longer alone. Trothan's father was there, wrapping his arms around her, resting his head for a moment on her shoulder. But she remained rigid. Maggie imagined he was nudging her with words too. Then he parted from her, stood next to her, raised his fists and threw one forward as if trying to fight the sea or the sky. He folded at the waist, head down, arms wrapping himself.

By the time she reached them, the pair were side-by-side

staring at a sea prickling with rainfall. Maggie stopped. She could hear the man breathing next to her, drawing in and out, overlaying the breathing of the sea. Her own lungs seemed to slow.

She watched the waves, the froth-flecked water and its characteristic red tide of algae. Alarm flashed through her. What if a body had been found? She turned and asked: 'Is there any news?'

'No,' the father turned slightly towards her and she looked into his wide, wrinkle-scarred face. He seemed to struggle for words, raised his hands slightly, dabbing at the air.

There was a murmur then from the woman behind him. Words that prickled with madness, rose in volume, turned a blade of blame towards Maggie. He cast back some quiet words, turning to his wife with his hands outstretched.

Beyond the man, Maggie heard the crisp shift of Nora's coat, saw a red shape flurrying past him. Nora hurtled two or three strides towards Maggie and two palms banged hard on her chest, knocking breath out of her as she overbalanced and fell onto the wet sand, an elbow breaking her fall. She sat up quickly, crawled onto her knees. A swipe came across the side of her head, clumsy and fleshy, but hard enough to topple and dizzy her. A flailing body was now above and around Maggie, blows pounding onto her shoulders and arms, each one accompanied by a grunt of effort.

'Hey, hey,' the Father's voice was loud, close behind the red fury.

And then the blows receded.

Squinting round from her slump on the sand, Maggie saw he had caught Nora from behind in a bear-hug, trapping her arms between his own. He was crooning, 'Nora, Nora.'

Maggie scrambled up and recovered her footing, but remained unbalanced. She began to walk backwards and away, unable to take her eyes off the mother and father, screwing up everything towards understanding. All she had done was help the child with a map.

The man had turned his wife in his arms so she was against him, his face hidden against her neck. Maggie glimpsed Nora's face, screwed up and red. Sobs erupted from the joined heart of the couple as they receded into a single perpendicular against the grey line of the horizon. They rocked and heaved in a slow dance that ran with rain onto the mirrored beach, apparently oblivious to their soaking and their isolation.

A gull cried out loud above Maggie. She clamped her hands over her ears as it wailed on and on. And she willed it not to blend with the rising note of a mother's long haunting scream. She turned and ran.

EIGHTEEN

Starting down the lane for home a few days later, Maggie glanced in at the driveway of the bungalow and saw Sally's face at a window. A frown flashed across it. Then Sally disappeared.

Two cars were parked near Flotsam Cottage and as she approached them Maggie realised each one was occupied; a figure low in the seat as if they'd been there a long while, each bowing their head over a small slab of smart phone. The heads bobbed up and she saw the flicker of a hand rising to a door next to her, heard it swing open, gravel scraping under a boot. Her name was called from behind her in an educated Edinburgh voice.

A second car door slamming.

She pictured dictaphones with little red lights going on in their pockets as they strode towards her; Carol picking up a copy of the Daily Mail somewhere and recognising her sister's back on page five – something in the set of her neck, the short but messily growing out hairstyle. She walked quickly into her drive and for the first time closed the wrought iron gates behind her. Looking quickly back up the lane, she glimpsed Sally hovering in her own gateway beyond the cars, looking towards her.

Her hands shook so much on the key that it took a long while to unlock the door. From the window she saw two heads meeting behind the hedge where the lane ran, heard a smatter of conversation, then car doors slamming in turn. Maggie put down her bag of food. Even when she heard the cars rattling the stones on the lane as they left, she was unable to relax. She hovered like a moth behind closed curtains. She knew they'd be back.

Bits of Maggie's statement had already appeared in the press, and she'd been mentioned in headlines. She wasn't sure which was worse; the ones that ignored her role in the boy's life or the ones that implicated her in some way: 'Missing Boy's "Lady Friend" Questioned'; 'Incomer Questioned Over Boy's Disappearance'. No one except her had deserved a headline of their own just for being questioned.

'You're just going to have to stick it out, the paparazzi,' Carol said. 'They'll get bored pretty soon if you ignore them.'

She accepted the advice, but Carol could have no idea what it felt like to be cornered. Under siege, Maggie fingered the bruises on her arms, brooding confirmation of the accusations gathering against her.

The proofs came back from Richard, leaving her a week to submit print-ready PDF files. She was shocked by the number of corrections needed, the careless slips she'd made. There was a lot to do. A week at the computer. Typos and more. The line of a river had risen above a place name text, and somehow the Osun-Osogbu Sacred Grove had uprooted itself and slipped over the border into Benin. She was embarrassed by her lack of professional care. But once again, the irony of her remote map-making struck her. If she'd actually walked through the shade of the Sacred Grove and breathed in its resiny scents, such an error never could have happened.

She stayed indoors. Her only connection beyond the walls was through Carol's persistent phone calls which now brought memories clamouring at the doors and windows.

'Do you remember Dad's library?' Maggie said.

There was a silence. 'Of course. But why now?'

'I was just thinking about it.'

'Why?'

'When we cleared the house. Afterwards.'

Maggie felt again the precious heft of her father's books as she took them off the shelves one by one and put them into boxes, fragmenting the unique arrangement of titles. The spines of his atlases, maps, novels, travel and geology books chimed and rhymed with each other: *The World Atlas of Wine* next to *Grapes of Wrath* next to *Look Back in Anger* next to a map of *Angers*. When she put them into boxes, his playful poetry was destroyed. It felt like dismantling a life brick by brick, stripping the family house of this piece of personal history which had characterised her father's study; the curiosities he'd collected over a lifetime of geography teaching and an interest in literature.

She wondered if Carol had even been aware how painful it had been for her to do this. She'd been tied up with young children, distracted by feeds and nappies and 'getting the house done and dusted and onto the market'.

'What's that got to do with anything now, Maggie?' Carol asked.

It was obvious to Maggie that her current loss was hauling up others, hand-over-hand. Her father's guttering breath as his head turned finally away from her; his books sent off to some sale or other. Maggie's whole body seemed lead-weighted with the ache of it even though her father had been buried now for eight years.

'I don't know,' she said. 'Just remembering, I suppose.'

The next morning she started to make the final corrections to the atlas, but then after an hour or so jumped up, made coffee, paced between the windows, the curtains drawn back again. The trees outside were heavy with leaf, parting with the wind to reveal the sea and snatches of reddish cliff on Dunnet Head. Despite her confinement, it was strange to think that waves would still be pounding onto the beach; the humid huff of the laundry breathing over the village.

She turned away, persuading herself to settle to her work. She only had a few days left. She went to the kitchen instead.

Turning on the oven, she started to cream together sun-softened butter and brown sugar, broke two eggs into it, flour and chocolate powder. She turned it into a tin and put it in the oven. The 30 minutes it took to bake would keep her here and the aroma would leach out of the house, seek out Trothan wherever he was, draw him in. She opened a window. Surely the scent would at least reach the woods. Then she took the cake from the oven and rested it on a cooling tray, knowing it would never be eaten.

The boy had always had a spectral weightlessness about him, an insubstantiality. It wasn't just that he didn't have a contemporary child's existence – no mobile phone, no clinging to a computer or even the handlebars of a stunt bike. His footing on the earth seemed invisible; the small nests he'd made of feathers, grasses, mussel shells were ephemeral. He would easily disappear.

It sometimes seemed she had conjured him from her imagination. But she reminded herself of his pungent presence, how she'd brushed specks of sand from the top of his damp head. He especially seemed real when she examined her bruises. Those thumps were evidence. That hulk of a red-faced woman had been feeling something tangible. Even if it did seem to be too late.

Another day came. She left the house cautiously, walked up and down the garden looking towards the bay. Then she went back inside, leaned over Trothan's map, refocusing on each place to see if she'd overlooked something.

'Are you missing Oxford?' Carol asked her.

'Yes,' Maggie said automatically. She didn't even know she had been, but her eyes smarted as she thought of her old, safe desk between Richard and the bay window looking out on the river; her evenings watching art house movies; going to talks and lectures; the narrow streets. The other 'her'. An old familiarity seemed to tug her south, as if she would re-inhabit her life as it had once been. As if she could go back.

'At least Dad's not witnessing this,' Carol said.

'What do you mean?'

'He'd have been distraught. To see you getting yourself into… To see you going through this.'

Another day came and she succumbed to work, finally establishing a rhythm. Her application to it reminded her of the months after the accident when work had been a refuge of sorts. When a chasm of time had to be filled with something.

She made bread in her breaks. It was a relief to do something physical; to pound the dough under her hands, to think, and in particular to consolidate her ideas about Lagos. She'd watched a series of short films made by young Lagosians and played back in her head some of the vox-pop voices: 'You're alive? You gotta be in Lagos.'; 'You wake up running. No one's chasing though.'

The enchantment was palpable in the look in their dreamy eyes and wide grins. 'It turns you into a monster – won't let you go!'

The city came alive to her with breath and clamour, sucking in streams of people who were escaping something or had been lured to a honey-pot of possibilities, the promise of new life. It spread itself to embrace outlying villages and laid bare its transformational power, roaring out music, leading trends in art and fashion, flaunting big business for the world's attention. She tried to think of a simple way of representing this, concentrating now on what Trothan would have done. *How did you do that?* A shrug: *I just saw it in my head.* If only she could have asked him.

Other absences reared up in her memory. Frank getting into the driving seat of his car and disappearing towards Reading. He'd moved out comprehensively, but for days afterwards a half-used packet of Tesco's ham lay in the fridge. She didn't eat ham; it was his. She left it there, the top slice darkening and curling with time, the sell-by date a reminder of his day of leaving. He also left a ring of dark filaments around the bath, as if he'd shed a coat before he left for his new life. And there were the wedding presents, the crockery bought on their holidays, the gloves, ornaments and books that could never properly be severed from memories of him. They had gradually composted to the lower depths of drawers and cupboards until she harvested them for jumble sales.

'Have you been to the police again?' Carol asked.

'They came to me.' Kept coming.

'And do you have any idea?' Carol asked.

'The parents seem convinced he's not coming back.'

'Oh Maggie, it's all so odd. Do you think it's them, then?'

'Them?'

'Who're responsible.'

Although Maggie was gratified by this idea, she knew it wasn't credible. 'Through neglect maybe,' she said, then added: 'They seem to blame me.'

There was a long pause, and then Carol said, 'Maggie, I think you'd better come home.'

Carol still seemed to cling to the idea that Maggie was having a little holiday that she would return from when she was ready.

'You know you've no reason to stay away, don't you?' Carol ventured, caution adding a strained note to her voice. 'Your sacrifice won't bring that little girl back. Or mend her parents' marriage.'

Maggie felt the old sting in her stomach. To be away from this place was unthinkable anyway. 'No, I don't think so.'

Carol, gently now: 'Shall I come there? I could get away at the weekend?'

Maggie wanted company, but did she want this?

'I have to say, Maggie. I did think the set-up you had was pretty strange. Such an odd boy.'

'No,' Maggie said.

'Sorry?'

'No. Don't come. I'm fine.'

'But you've no one to talk to.'

'Graham's kind to me.'

'Graham?'

'Yes,' Maggie said. 'Remember. You met him at the bird centre.'

'I know. Isn't he married?'

'So?'

Carol hesitated. 'You're not getting yourself into more bother, are you?'

Maggie put the phone down soon afterwards.

No one called. Trothan had been her only visitor. And then the police. But now that nine days had passed since his disappearance, they seemed to have finished with her and no one was keeping her informed. The boy continued to suggest himself around the cottage; a scattering of sand and hair, hints of salt and pollen, a slight scent of woodsmoke. Sometimes she heard a voice rising, lilting in a far away corner of the house; but it always transformed into a bird calling from the rooftop. The always-present absence. Like a packet of ham left in the fridge.

Frank had been the one to help her clear her father's house. He'd salvaged a book of nursery rhymes that her father had himself once read to her.

'Let's keep it,' Frank had said, holding it out to her. But when she took it, he didn't let go of his end. With the book held between them they conceived in their minds the children they would console with stories and rhymes after their first losses – teeth, hamsters, grandparents. They had smiled at each other, making a contract without words.

Maggie submitted all the final PDF files to Richard.

'Time to celebrate soon,' came back his email.

Very funny, she snarled back in her thoughts.

Hunger and an empty fridge now snapped her from her caged circling. She took a deep breath and strode from the house, locking the door behind her. Defiant. Leaping the barricades. No one was waiting for her in the lane.

She went to the village. Walking along the main street, she anticipated mothers gathering their children against themselves, an elbow-clamp of safety around their necks. She felt they would do it unconsciously as they stood chatting on the pavements with other parents; the closing army of the righteous all touched by a threat to their own children. She could see why they might regard her with suspicion: a woman alone who deliberately chose to make her best friend a child.

'Hormones,' they'd be whispering behind her. What had she done with him?

A big static caravan for the incident room had been deposited in the centre of the village next to the playpark, opposite the shop. The door was open and a policewoman was visible inside, standing with a clipboard, presumably in case anyone should remember anything. A roadside sign, visible in both directions to passing traffic, asked: 'Have you seen this child?' under a huge image of Trothan tamed by a camera flash in his blue school sweatshirt, hair brushed back unnaturally behind his ears.

She was standing staring at it when Audrey appeared at her side, rustling shopping bags.

'Maggie?'

Audrey brought the school in her wake like a following fog; the awful memory of that evening two weeks before which was the last time they'd seen each other. What platitudes could they exchange now?

'That's just not him,' Maggie muttered at Trothan's photo.

'Sorry?' Audrey said.

Maggie nodded at the photo and said, 'school doesn't suit him.' Then mumbled an apology.

Audrey laughed, didn't take offence. 'I'm not sure he suited us either.'

Maggie bit her lip when she heard the past tense. Surely they hadn't all given up on him quite so soon?

There was a flurry at the incident room door.

Audrey looked across. 'Better go.'

'More questions?'

Audrey nodded. 'You've seen them, I assume?'

'Several grillings,' Maggie said.

Audrey walked away and then turned back mid-stride and cocked her head with an attempt at a smile. 'I expect we all feel a little responsible.'

Maggie looked at her feet. When she looked up, Audrey's back was disappearing into the caravan.

It was then that she noticed a headline on the hoarding outside the shop:

'FISHERMAN HAD ILLEGAL GUN TO SHOOT SEALS'

She hurried inside, bought a copy of the *John O'Groats Journal*, and read:

'Quarrytown fisherman Jim Swanson has been charged with illegal ownership of a firearm discovered by missing schoolboy Trothan Gilbertson. It's believed the boy found it in Quarrytown's disused church, property of local builder Rab McNicholl. The fisherman is suspected of using the gun to shoot seals sometimes held responsible for decimating the fish population. Bail has been granted. The man is also under investigation for the sale of illegally landed fish.'

'Open secret,' Graham said about the fish sales when she went to the Centre. 'He didn't worry too much about sticking to his quota. They were all in on it. No surprises there.'

'Even me,' she said. 'Except I was too naïve to realise.'

He studied her face as if looking for the tern scar on her forehead. 'At this rate I'd better keep a bottle of whisky in my desk drawer for you,' he said.

'What do you mean?'

'All these licks you seem to take on the beach.'

'Nora,' she said. 'You saw?'

Graham nodded. 'I tried to catch you afterwards, but you ran the other way.'

Maggie felt her breathing crank up a notch, wondered vaguely why he looked out for her like this, and whether she wanted him to. He delivered her a cup of plastic tea in his shaky hand, and led her outside so he could have a cigarette.

'Why's Nora got it in for you, anyway?'

Maggie turned away slightly. 'Jealous maybe?'

'Because the lad was attached to Flotsam Cottage?'

'What do you mean?'

'Kept turning up at the door, eh?'

She stood up, walked a few steps towards the sea. Breathed the comment away. Concentrated on calm. She hadn't wanted to contemplate that Trothan might only have been visiting her because of a failure to readjust back home.

'Is there any news?' Graham asked from behind her.

She returned to the bench. 'They seem to have given him up for lost.'

'No sign, then?' Graham asked.

She shook her head.

'Strange, how the parents gave him such a long leash, considering their troubles getting a bairn in the first place.'

'Oh?'

'My missus says if you're fit, there's a better chance of conceiving. As well as not smoking. Oops,' he hid the hand holding his cigarette below the bench. 'So maybe George was trying to lose weight. Every day for a year he walked the beach.'

'A year?'

'I always saw him at first light even on the coldest of days, even when the beach was white with snow. He'd get to the rocks at Dunnet and turn around.'

'And then Trothan came along?'

Graham nodded. 'No one ever seemed to know that Nora was pregnant. But I suppose there's room for a bit of a disguise, eh?'

They both stared out to the gun-metal horizon.

'The police have been, then?' she asked.

'They've interviewed everyone, haven't they? The school, neighbours, bus drivers, ferry ports.'

'Did they ask about me?'

He nodded.

'What?' she asked.

'Did I know you.' He paused.

'And?'

'What did I know about your relationship with Trothan.'

'And you said?'

Graham shrugged. 'Just that you took an interest in him and his talents.' He took a drag on his cigarette. 'I seem to be the only witness.'

'To my "relationship" with him?'

'I mean the only person to see the lad that morning.'

Maggie swung around to look at him. 'When?'

'Apart from you, I mean.'

'You saw him on the beach? Are you sure it was him?'

'From up there, aye.' Graham indicated the upstairs look-out. 'I was in stupidly early that day before heading out to Bettyhill.'

'What was he doing?'

'He was ploutering about on the edge of the surf. Way down there. But I could see it was him because of the long hair flapping about. Didn't think much of it till the news went up.'

She stared at him.

He turned and met her gaze. 'I'm not going to feel bad about it, Maggie. He was aye wandering about on his own at odd times.'

Maggie was wrestling for explanations, and arrived now at one for George and Nora's confrontation with the sea when she'd last seen them.

'He had something wrapped about him,' Graham said. 'Against the wind, I suppose.'

'What sort of something?'

Graham shrugged. 'Too far away to see. A big coat, maybe.'

'You think he'll turn up again?'

Graham shrugged. 'It's only a few days, eh?'

'Two weeks now,' Maggie said. 'And by the way it was the sealskin I found in the loft.'

'What was?'

'That he had draped around him. I gave it to him that morning.'

'Good move. That'll keep him cosy, wherever he is. He's maybe using some of his bushcraft skills to lay low a while.'

'You don't think he went into the sea, then?'

'It was a high surf. It's not in a child's nature to be suicidal, is it?'

'Where would a body end up?'

'That's a morbid question, isn't it?' Graham said, taking a puff on his cigarette. 'If it hopped aboard the North Atlantic Current from here, might end up in the Arctic Circle somewhere.' He gestured to his right, northwards.

Maggie didn't reply.

He lowered the binoculars. 'You'll need to stop beating yourself up, you know.'

She nodded vaguely, keeping her eyes out to sea.

'Look at it like this. He's as likely got in a car with someone or fallen in a hole, or...'

'Stop,' she said. 'That's... too cruel.'

He patted her knee. 'Let's face it, it's likely no one'll ever really know.'

She thought for a moment, wondered how to try something out on him. 'But what if it wasn't like that?'

Graham stubbed his cigarette out, turned to her, frowning. 'What do you mean?'

She was thinking of the day she'd brought Carol here, the stories he'd talked about. 'What if he was "going back"?' she said tentatively. 'Escaping human hurts.'

He chuckled, and when she didn't join in he looked at her and his face sank. 'Are you serious?'

'It happened on the solstice, the longest day.'

'So?' He scratched his ear in an irritable way, then slapped his thighs and stood up.

'A coincidence, don't you think?' she insisted.

Graham didn't react, looked vaguely in the direction of the door to the Centre as if checking for visitors.

'It's when things happen, isn't it?' she said.

'Things?' he looked back at her now.

Maggie nodded, unwilling to spell it out any further.

His pale eyes held hers then, unblinking. He seemed to be trying to retrieve something. 'Well, I mind him coming in and reading about those selkie stories we've got on the wall, right enough. But he surely knew they were just stories? Any child that age has grown out of Santa and all that.'

She continued to look at him, and he began to frown.

'Who'd put an idea like that into the child's head?' he asked eventually. 'That he could swim away; turn himself into a seal?'

She pictured then Trothan's drawing of the seals, noses down, pirouetting into free, wide waters. Finding space. Escape.

After a long silence, Graham said kindly, 'I'm taking a wee group to Duncansby Stacks later if you want to come along?'

NINETEEN

Returning to the cottage from the shop a week or so later, she saw that someone was hovering near her door, hand outstretched as if knocking at it. She didn't recognise Sally at first in a smart green coat, belted at the waist, formal, as if she was going somewhere important.

Maggie smiled as she approached, genuinely pleased to see a friendly face, and stretched past Sally to open the door wide. 'Come in.'

But Sally didn't move, stayed put on the decking, so that Maggie ended up half-in and half-out of the door.

'I won't stop, thanks,' Sally said. 'I just wanted to give you this.'

An envelope was in Maggie's hand; her name on it but no address. Hand-delivered.

'I didn't want to just put it through your door without saying anything.' There was a pinkish flush to Sally's face, a hand tugging some stray hair behind her ear.

Maggie stared at the envelope.

'We have to do it like this, just keeping things straight legally when a lease is about to expire.'

Maggie nodded, suddenly understanding. A formality. She ripped open the envelope, expecting to see a contract; the next six months' lease with a dotted line for her signature.

'Are you sure you won't have a coffee?' she asked as she unfolded the page.

But then she engaged properly, frowned down on a letter; a reminder that the lease would expire on the last day of August, six months after it had started, and in only six weeks' time. She turned the paper over but it was blank.

'It is renewable, isn't it?' Maggie remembered discussing this in the phone calls before she'd signed up and moved in: 'All being well, on both sides,' Sally had volunteered. At the time Maggie hadn't been able to think beyond six months; she'd expected to be searching out the next white space on the map by then.

But now Sally hesitated. 'Not this time, I'm afraid.' She offered no further explanation. No family members in need of a home; no essential repairs that required the cottage to be empty.

Maggie looked at Sally, conjuring up behind her the McNicholls hauled there by Brutus; Black Fish Jim in his yellow wellies somehow in less disgrace than her; Small and Anderson; George; and of course Nora who was triumphant and red-clawed. The village gathering in sullen rows. They paused in a moment of still regard for her before starting to ebb, dissipate, break away into factions.

Out of nowhere a yearning swooped inside her. A yearning for a winter here, for an exchange of birds, some shoaling south and others arriving from the north. She would have welcomed the change. Long shadows. The scent of ice just to the north. The wood-burning stove would have roared through long nights. Fragments of stone, bone, shell would gather with feathers on the hearth. She'd hang pictures on the wall. It would be a growing life, weighted to anchor her properly here. Quite a different kind of weight to the one she'd been dragging around like a ball and chain.

Her focus came back onto Sally, the sole representative of the village in her official green coat, who then apologised, turned, and drifted away from Maggie's still-open door.

Maggie walked to the beach with her head down. In the days since last seeing Graham she stayed at the Quarrytown end and didn't go as far as the Centre. He seemed to have joined everyone in consigning Trothan to the deep; the search apparently scaled down. Their 'deep' might have been abduction or drowning or a plummeting mine shaft. But it amounted to the same thing. It was nothing like the deep she pictured for him in which he remained living and might still return.

Today the sea had retreated further than she'd ever seen it. Spring tides again. Extreme rising; extreme falling. She'd been staring at the sea's surface in the last weeks, trying to imagine, to see as the child had done, what lay beneath; the old fishermen's dying maps. But all she got back was reflected light, the fleet shadows of seabirds skimming the mirror and then dissolving beneath. She wondered what they charted. Wrecks, fish-traps, engagement rings and contraband; soft coral fingers pointing upwards from the deepest rocks.

But now the vast surface was peeled back, the 'beneath' revealed: sand wrinkled by small currents, heaped with kelp and dotted with the lugworms' curled castles of sculpted mud; a landscape new and unfamiliar to her. It seemed like the foreboding of a tsunami, the lurch of sea back towards the horizon. Birds were grounded by the event, stalking the mud, flightless and silenced.

Her shoes were off, her bare feet soon numbed by wading the pools caught between grey strands. The flat, bright no man's land stretched around her and the dunes fell back as she moved beyond the cartographer's 'blue line' showing what was un-mappable beyond the tide. She was traversing both water and land. If she went further she might come across the downed spitfire and find herself sharing the territory of seals.

As if sucked out by the moon's lure; as if called towards a distant singing heard through folding valleys, she continued. Under her feet strange crevasses gaped, oozing grey residues. She wandered on, feet slick, back turned on what she knew, towards the horizon.

TWENTY

Trothan's map was already on the wall of the cottage. She'd been surprised that no-one had asked for it back, but she certainly wasn't going to offer it. At least the details exposed on it would surely now be acted upon. How could the archaeologists ignore the desecrated Viking grave, or the police not investigate the illegal removal of sand and shooting of seals?

She tore out the local page from the Road Atlas with its few lines for roads, its occasional settlements, its exaggerated white spaces within the cat's-head outline of the coast. She found a smaller frame for it so it could hang next to Trothan's for her remaining days; the map that had called her here. She hammered a nail directly into Sally's pristine white wall, each bang a small, fierce thrill.

The rest of the Road Atlas now stayed on her table. She flicked through it as she ate breakfast, turning west to Ullapool which looked remote and was far enough away that her story might not pursue her there. She turned over another wad of pages. Manchester. A scream of colour and line. The other end of the atlas; North Devon, perhaps. If the car could get that far.

She couldn't yet settle to work on the new project. There was always a period after a deadline when relief and sadness mingled; the accelerating activity followed by a hiatus. But this wasn't just inertia.

One afternoon about six weeks after Trothan's disappearance Graham came to the cottage to find her. He'd been at the pier at Dwarwick when the boat came in; the men had been putting out creels for lobsters.

She gasped when he told her and sank onto the sofa, head in her hands. Graham came and sat next to her, his body heat reaching her even through the crackle of his waterproof. He said nothing at first, then: 'Breathe, Maggie. Breathe.'

'You said he'd probably fallen down a hole,' she finally said.

'Aye, well. Looks like I was wrong.'

It was one of his wellies. Just one. Faded blue. The white daisies dancing across it. They'd found it washed up under the cliffs on Dunnet Head. She bit back all her 'buts'; realised it wasn't worth questioning what it meant. Graham had come specifically to tell her. And now the Fairy Godmother's spell had been comprehensively broken; the coach horses returned to rats. And she was being drummed out of the place which connected her to the child.

Graham made her a cup of tea; searched the cottage unsuccessfully for whisky. She stayed on the sofa. Graham tried to get her to speak but her head was a deep murmuring pit. Eventually he had to leave for the long drive home.

'Are Sally and Nora friends?' She asked him just as he was going out of the door.

He shrugged, frowned. 'They'll know each other of course. Boys in the same class; both oddballs in a way.'

'So Sally was doing Nora a favour when she let her move in

here?'

Graham laughed, clearly keen to leave now. 'I've no idea. Why does it matter?'

'Just wondering.' The collusion seemed obvious to Maggie. Sally had been a placid, welcoming woman and was now evicting her under Nora's dark charm.

After Graham left, Maggie didn't move from the sofa, numbed by a dead-weight. The ticks from her watch told her of time passing, but measured it in sickening distortions. Twenty minutes, according to its face, occupied what felt like a whole day.

She moved in the early evening to lie fully-clothed on the bed. Dusk brought the cackles of crows to the high trees outside. Nora's face bore down on her; wings, horns, a tail tucked back behind her.

At ten, in an attempt to disentangle herself, she phoned Carol.

'She attacked me,' Maggie finally blurted. 'On the beach, the last time I saw her.'

There was a silence then: 'Physically?'

'Yes. I had bruises for weeks.'

Carol's voice came slowly, words carefully manoeuvred, 'And I assume you reported it to the police?'

'No.'

'Why not?'

It had never occurred to Maggie to do so. Perhaps she'd believed herself in some way deserving of it. Not now though. Not now, as she surged upright in bed. 'I'd hit back. Now. If I could.' The image came of her hands on Nora's face; her fingers plunging into bloody places. Then she was on her feet, pacing the room, breathing erratically into the phone.

'Maggie,' Carol crooned, reducing her to a hurt child.

Maggie took a deep breath. 'If she'd been a proper mother in the first place...'

'Maggie,' Carol came again. 'It might be hard for you to understand, because...'

Maggie waited.

'It's primeval. That mother's defence.'

'The attack?'

'I'd probably do the same. Probably capable of it. If...'

'If what?' screeched Maggie. 'If someone tried to help your child? When you couldn't be bothered?'

'Calm down.' Words curt now, less patient. 'I know why you're taking it so personally, obviously, but I assume others there won't know why.'

Maggie was speechless.

'Just keep away from her, eh? She's grieving.'

'And I'm not?'

'She'll always be grieving now. And she could be a danger to you.'

Maggie's hands were shaking so much the phone rattled as she put it back into its stand. Her stomach was a raw wound, and all Carol had done was salt it. She returned to bed, jittered through the dark, ambushed by dreams which she escaped from into a half-waking state. She heard the ghastly grinding of her own teeth.

By the time dawn came, Maggie at least knew one thing. She wasn't going to leave without facing Nora. Sleeplessness had made a blade of her.

The phone rang just as she was about to leave the house. She hovered over it for three rings and then grabbed it to her ear;

listened.

'Maggie?'

'Yes, Richard,' she said.

'That was strange.'

'What?'

'I didn't hear you speak.'

'I didn't.'

Richard paused for a moment. 'You okay?'

Maggie took a breath, trying to pull herself back a little from the path she was already striding. 'Just a little distracted,' she said. 'Sorry.'

'I hadn't heard from you in such a long time, thought I'd just see if there's anything you need from me.'

'Right.'

'I guess you'll be in the thick of your summer visitors, all lured up to the seaside?'

She puffed out a breath of amusement at this idea. 'Something like that.'

There was a pause. Maggie glimpsed waves through the trees below the cottage churning towards the dunes.

'Must be lovely at this time of year,' Richard said. 'I've always meant to get up to John O'Groats myself. Been to Land's End enough times.'

'I haven't forgotten,' Maggie said, trying to collect herself. 'About the new project. Despite the distractions.'

'No problem,' Richard said. 'Just touching base, as I say. West Africa'll be rolling off the press soon. We'll have to celebrate. Need to get you down for the next editorial meeting anyway.'

'Sorry Richard. But I'd better go.' And then searching for an excuse, 'Doctor's appointment.'

'Sure,' he said. 'You're okay?'

'I'm okay,' she said, and was quickly on her way.

This time she knocked when she reached their door, didn't walk in as she had before. Her heart chattered in her chest and her mouth felt dry. She half-hoped that no one would be in.

She was about to turn away when the door opened a crack. The darkness inside against August's brilliance gave nothing away, and she entertained a fantasy that it was Trothan opening the door; that he'd returned and no one had told her. But when the door opened a little more, she saw that it was George, wearing a fisherman's-style jumper with a frayed neck. She was glad it wasn't Nora.

It was the first time she'd seen him since the incident on the beach. If she'd passed him on the street, a red-eyed and droop-faced stranger, she'd have guessed he was an alcoholic. He ran a hand over the top of his head, eyes on the mat. When he looked up there was no trace of animosity. It was more like a baffled enquiry.

'Could I speak to Nora?' she blurted.

He looked at her for a few seconds without speaking. 'You'll have heard?'

Some sort of fluff had got attached to the stubble on his chin and it made her think of Trothan with feathers caught in his hair. It triggered an impulse to reach out and straighten him up.

She nodded, muttered, 'I'm really sorry.'

A minute or so passed in which they each seemed to withdraw and yet stayed where they were. A gauze of time stretching between them. A windless calm. There was something bear-like about this man. An embrace with him, she imagined, would be both abrasive and soft, scented with woodsmoke and this morning's bacon. She could picture him with a tiny baby bundled in his arms. Outside. On the beach would be right. He'd smile down at a pink face, his hand larger than the child's head that it cupped.

'Look,' he said. 'A bitty time's passed now. I'm sorry for that – you know,' he nodded in the direction of the sea. 'On the beach that day.'

'It's okay.' Maggie said. 'I just wanted to speak to her.'

'She's not here.'

Like a door slamming. Eyes shutting against her. A refusal.

'When will she be back?' asked Maggie.

George shrugged. 'Like I said...' But he didn't seem quite able to make a sentence. 'We're just getting...'

Maggie knew that he couldn't possibly mean 'back to normal.' She started to turn away, driven by common courtesy, a doorway narrowing, George's face receding. But she couldn't now just turn tail in defeat. She swung back to face the door, the lit stripe of face. As if in response, it opened a little again.

'Sorry, but. Where is she?'

'Aye, she's on her own just now,' he said gently, stepping more fully into the gap.

'I'd like to know where she is.' She was surprised by the sound of her own boldness.

George repeated the sweep of his hand over his head. With a kick in the gut, the idea arrived with Maggie that Nora might have left him.

'She goes...' he waved his hand vaguely. 'Every day. Where she gets a wee bitty sense of connection.'

Maggie bit her lip. Did he mean the beach?

'I don't go,' he said. 'Don't want to get in the way. It's a mother thing maybe.'

She heard the warning. 'Okay.'

Maggie thought it unlikely he was willing to say any more. She stepped backwards and simultaneously he did the same. The door between them clicked gently to. She turned, then, and walked back up the path to her bicycle. Barely pausing to think, guided by a gut geography, she pointed the bike inland.

When she arrived at Saint Trothan's, Mobility Man was parked at the wrought-iron gate on his scooter; a fluorescent slump over a cigarette. She leant her bicycle against the wall under the dark shade of the trees and greeted him. He squinted at her, not moving except for the slow rise of the cigarette to his mouth, nodding with his head a-cock.

'Anyone else inside?' She peered over his head into the graveyard where stones leaned and tree-shaped shadows writhed across the grass.

Mobility Man looked vaguely over his shoulder. 'Aye,' he said, as if the answer was complete in itself.

Maggie's instinct had brought her towards this miniature heart of moss and stone. Bone and leaf. A place which rang out Trothan's name even though it couldn't provide a resting place for his body.

'Have you finished your map yet?' Mobility Man asked.

She was confused. Was he referring to the maps for the book she'd submitted back in June? Had she even mentioned that to him when they'd sat on the water's edge talking about a dead seal? Or perhaps he was talking about Trothan's map, which would never exactly be complete now.

'Well, I've been to most places around here now, if that's what you mean.'

He nodded as if in satisfaction.

It was a kind of mapping she'd been doing, she supposed. She was like a Victorian explorer going somewhere for as long as it took to fill the white spaces on the map, and then moving on, adopting on the way a different hairstyle perhaps, or hair-colour, a whole reinvention of herself for a new place, as Carol would accuse her.

'Well,' she said, moving as if to get around his scooter to the gate that he seemed almost wedged up against.

'You'll not want to go in,' he snapped at her.

'Oh?'

He nodded his head behind him through the gate. 'It's her that brings herself here every day. The mother.' Tight-lipped on the cigarette, his eyes pinched shut and then opened on her. 'Miss seeing him about the place. He and I. Two lost souls wandering about.'

Make that three, thought Maggie.

'Terrible thing that – no grave to visit,' he said.

'Is your wife buried here?' Maggie asked.

He nodded across the road to another gate which she knew opened onto a new, neatly regimented cemetery. 'Come every day, just like that wifie back there. That's why they gave me the scooter – too far from the village.'

Maggie peered over his shoulder again but couldn't see anyone amongst the old gravestones. She could walk away now and never see Nora again. She'd never spoken to Lizzie Ginner's family, never even written to them, despite the number of letters she'd started. She'd never sought forgiveness or tried to be involved in their grief. It was the Get-On-With-Your-Life practicality of advisers such as Carol that had won the day. But she'd begun to wonder if that was the best way.

She took a decisive stride, wriggled past the scooter and unlatched the gate.

'Nice to see you again,' she said with a sense of partial triumph as she re-latched it from inside and turned towards the darkest clusters of iron, ivy, stone and shade at the far end of the graveyard. As she padded across the grass, she heard the scooter start up and whine away, back towards the village.

As Maggie stepped into the doorway of the roofless church, her shadow loomed over Nora who was sitting on the mossy ground on a folded newspaper. She seemed to be writing in a small notebook. Maggie noticed that the colour on her perfectly manicured nails had grown out; they were just tipped with scarlet. Nora looked up with a start that wobbled her face and the flesh on her bare upper arms.

'Sorry,' Maggie said. 'To intrude.'

Nora stared at her.

Maggie saw, as she had in George, a physical change. All the hard, cow-horn strength that Maggie had been prepared for had gone. She looked crumpled.

As if realising this herself, Nora now dropped the book and pencil, flopped onto her hands and knees and started scrabbling to get herself upright, until she was facing Maggie with her arms hanging at her sides.

'I wanted to speak to you,' Maggie said, keen to break the silence.

'If it's an apology you're after...?'

'No,' Maggie said quickly.

The insomniac night that had driven her here now seemed inadequate preparation for all the possible things she could say; her certainty dissipated by daylight, the normality of Richard's call, George's soft underbelly exposed. Her undermined sense of purpose made her pre-prepared speech scarcely relevant. She took in the crumbly stone walls that enclosed them, this tiny place under a roof of swaying branches.

'Do you come here to pray?' she asked.

The bereaved left now to their loss: Lost.

'Call it that if you wish,' Nora said.

Maggie looked at the notebook and Nora stooped and picked it up, thrust it deep into a pocket as if Maggie might demand to see it. The skin around her lips was white, suggesting a tight line of force; her eyes averted.

Maggie moved backwards, almost unconsciously blocking the doorway again. 'My lease expires on the cottage soon.'

Nora nodded vaguely.

'I'm leaving.'

There was no response.

'I suppose you already knew?'

Nora made a slight gesture with her head and shoulders suggesting that it was neither here nor there.

Maggie wanted to mention Sally, suggest Nora's part in her eviction, but was lost for words. Another part of her steel-sure weaponry was failing to hit home.

'Why did you come to live here?' Nora suddenly asked.

'I'd every right.' Sweat prickling her armpits.

For the first time Nora darted a glance directly at Maggie. 'It was a genuine question. Why?'

Maggie thought for a moment, accepted she should answer honestly. 'For a change, I suppose.'

'And you've got it?'

Had she? She seemed to have become an expert at changing other people's lives. The hardest thing of all seemed to be to change herself, however much she tried. Her silence hung on too long for her to overcome it. She dropped to sitting on the step, hung her head between parted knees, a dead weight without sleep. Crows cawed above her in the trees.

Struggling to surface, Maggie eventually looked up. Nora was exactly where she'd been before, also apparently lost in thought.

'He won that competition by the way,' Maggie said. 'You probably won't remember.'

Nora was frowning now.

'The map-making one,' Maggie said. A letter had arrived for her the day before the welly was found.

'I don't think I got round to entering him.'

Maggie paused, and then said, 'I did.'

Nora stared at her. White skin taut around her mouth, blinking.

'I signed the form.'

Nora scrutinised Maggie's face. 'I see.'

'I've got the letter here, from the organisers. If you want it.' She started to forage in a pocket, eager to avoid Nora's gaze. She held it out, but Nora didn't move.

'Why would I want that?'

Maggie shrugged. 'He won.' It seemed that even now Nora was nonchalant about her son's talents. 'Surely any mother would be proud. It shows how remarkable he...' Maggie was silenced by a tussle between 'is' and 'was'.

Nora's eyes narrowed, reading correctly Maggie's dilemma. 'Exactly.' Her face heaved in an ugly twist against tears. 'You want to collect your glory, is that it?'

'No.'

'You really think your vanity matters?'

'Vanity?' Maggie felt a childish sob taking charge of her body. Even so her voice played back to her with whining melodrama; the shrill cry of uncertain conviction.

Nora put a hand on her forehead. She turned and faced the

wall, exposing her ugly, humpish back. Maggie began to think about leaving.

'It was a private thing,' Nora then said quietly, turning back.

Maggie waited.

'The way he came to us.'

Maggie heard in the strange expression an echo of Trothan's, 'I was their only gift'.

Nora continued. 'I came from a family of seven. I always wanted peace. That's why I started coming here as a child, with my homework and books.'

'You named him after it?'

Nora nodded. 'Never did me any harm, roaming about on my own. We didn't want to restrict him, draw too much attention to him, just because he was...' she was struggling for a word.

'Different?' Maggie ventured.

'...the only one. We didn't want him spoiled and wrapped in cotton wool. We loved his free spirit. We couldn't always be holding him back, capturing him for ourselves.'

Maggie wasn't sure if Nora was implying that she'd attempted to capture him.

Nora paused, breathing audibly, gulping her words. 'And now of course... we might think. We should have done it differently. There's many say we aren't, weren't, natural parents. You'll know that. But we were only ever his guardians.'

Nora parted her hands then and looked up, and for one mad moment, Maggie thought she might be included in that 'we', that gesture. And then it seemed to her it might be even more universal; the village, the whole bay as his guardians.

'I wasn't trying to spoil him, or give him too much attention,' Maggie said. 'Really I wasn't.' She registered that they were both now using the past tense. It had never occurred to her before that Nora and George might be blaming themselves for his disappearance.

'Why aren't you a mother?' Nora suddenly demanded.

Bang. Maggie caught her breath. A well-aimed strike, just when she thought they'd disarmed.

'It seems you'd like to be,' Nora said.

She could take all the blame, the blows raining down on her, the isolation, even her eviction. But she'd heard Nora's accusation. Childless women: selfish, unloving, and unable to understand just about anything about life.

Maggie flung herself onto her feet. Her blood surged, fingertips igniting with it, body hurled forward by the storm inside. She flew across the church, right fist clenching. Her arm muscles exploded to crash the fist against the oncoming wall.

She watched a scallop of sandstone shear off and float down onto the grass.

A gasp in of breath. Pain in the knuckles. The white look of bone amidst broken skin, then blood rising through it, bubbling up on the joints, dripping steadily onto the grass. And then she was crying, her back to Nora, head bent against the wall, shoulders heaving.

Minutes passed.

Her eyes closed.

The walls had shrunk around her. There was nothing. Nothing there.

'Here.'

She felt something close by, something soft on her torn, dripping hand. Nora was there patting a wad of tissues onto it.

'Take it,' she said. 'It needs pressure.'

Maggie drew away from the wall, pressed the wad onto her right hand with her left, nodding and wiping snot away with an arm. 'Thanks,' she managed.

Nora stepped away, was about to turn from her, and then said, 'And what I meant, was that you'd obviously like to be a...' She avoided the word that had been so charged. 'Because of how you were. With... the lad.'

She went away then, back to sitting on the folded newspaper, head bowed.

Maggie finally followed, sitting back on the step opposite, holding the bloody hand.

Nora looked up. 'It's stopping?'

Maggie nodded. 'Stupid,' she said. The pain was throbbing in now and she wondered if something was broken. She remained still, breathing hard.

'There's a few of us seem to have trouble,' Nora said, soft again.

'Trouble?'

'Conceiving.' Nora looked up. 'You were married?'

'That wasn't the trouble.'

'With the marriage?'

Maggie leant back against the stone doorway and took a deep breath. At that moment an explosive cry cackled at her back, and the shock unearthed her words, sent them spilling without thought: 'The trouble was with me.' A pheasant scuttering down to land just beyond the church door. She put a hand on her heart.

'What happened?' Nora asked.

Maggie bowed her head. Nora's direct question was like a dense force pressing in, breathing hot gusts on her neck. She didn't have to tell. But when she looked up, Nora was sitting with her back against the opposite wall, eyes averted and undemanding. She seemed, herself, incredibly exposed. Maggie felt the imbalance, saw that she owed something in this trading of griefs.

'She was just tiny.' Maggie bowed her head again. 'I was driving to work and had an accident. It was a girl.'

When Maggie drew breath and lifted her head, Nora was staring, her face salt-white. Maggie nodded. 'She died.'

It was as if Nora was re-living the pain for Lizzy Ginner's mother, delivering the hideous impact of the accident to Maggie yet again.

'How terrible,' Nora said.

Maggie drew in a deep breath, and a frail, coarse whisper came out. 'I know.' It had been held down without air for a long time in a chill, green place. 'I have asked myself many times since, please don't doubt it, whether I...'

'I meant,' Nora cut in. 'How terrible for you.'

Maggie held a breath. It burst from her as a small hiccupy sob of surprise. 'I couldn't stop. Not in time.'

'She stepped out?' Nora asked.

Maggie nodded. The thud and judder of the car, the reverberation through her foot on the brake pedal. She grimaced, her eyes clamped tight in an attempt to block it.

'Best put behind you, eh?'

'That's not easy,' Maggie said.

'But best,' Nora sounded almost motherly.

Maggie had the chance to escape now with the prize of sympathy. But she shook her head against this absolution, and then sensed Nora waiting. 'I don't remember very clearly, there are blanks, but I think...' She remembered the graze of her hair on her cheek; it had been too long then. She'd been tucking a stray loop of it back behind an ear. Hadn't she? She drew breath, and then said it: 'I think I was looking in the mirror.'

Nora let out an audible breath.

'Not for long, just a fraction of a second I'm sure, but maybe it was enough.'

Nora didn't look at her, just nodded.

'Vanity,' Maggie muttered, waving a hand at her hair, cut clear of her face now. 'You were right.'

Maggie dropped her head, sinking down.

Finally she felt Nora pass her, displacing a gust of warm air as she went back through the church door. At first Maggie thought that was it; Nora had left. She saw herself as if from above as she'd been at the scene of the accident; urine-soaked, standing apart. And now within this corner of the ruined church, she sat alone with bloody hands.

But when she glanced through the doorway she saw that Nora wasn't far away, standing still and looking down. Her humpish back no longer looked ridiculous but loaded her with a great burden of grief. Maggie took a deep breath and followed her, stood near her by the funny gravestone with its shimmering rock pool that reflected the tree-tossed sky but also suggested in its shadows anemones, kelp, crab-shells, the deep. They both stared down into it for a while before going their separate ways.

TWENTY
ONE

Maggie continued to prepare for her move. She gathered boxes, made sure the car would still run. She did a bit of work each morning, reported briefly on it to Richard to give him the appearance she was making progress. But her 'to do' list – tax the car, get more boxes, take meter readings – lay largely ignored on the table with the Road Atlas awaiting her decision.

She made it her priority to walk, often with a jagged rock of loss choking her throat; the sense that this might be her last time at each place.

She braved downpours, roaming the places Trothan had mapped as if she was saying goodbye to them; and perhaps through them, to him. She climbed Dwarwick Head to get the view of the pier below and the whole length of the Sands backed by the pyramid-shaped dunes. She found for the first time the well at what had once been a nunnery; visited the cave where the greedy man was chained with the Mermaid's wealth; and she returned to the derelict farm buildings and the lair. She even beat her way through nettles and brambles to find the tree trunk they'd crossed over the burn that day. And then she ignored a 'private' sign at the abandoned McNicholl church where she heard Brutus pacing and yelping inside. The paths she had helped to wear gave her some kind of right to these places and made the territory her own, just as they had belonged to the child.

Back at the cottage, with days shortening, her remaining time pressing in, she wanted to capture something. She found the Rotring pens that Trothan had left behind with the map on his last visit, chose the one with the 0.1 nib, noticing how its end was snagged by teeth marks. Experimentally she put it in her mouth, wanting to taste his salty life on it, and wondering if she would end up with a great black blob of ink on her own lips.

Despite a still sore, bandaged hand, she took a fresh page and drew a bird's eye view of Flotsam Cottage; put in a circle for the top of her own head. It felt strange to use a pen, to physically draw, after so long using a computer. And to do so in this way, with no layering, no attempt to balance space and clutter. In slow circles around the cottage she began to fill in details. She didn't consult Trothan's map; made this her own. It included the old reservoir and lade felled by age and gobbled by ivy, benches she'd sat on in the village, all the places she'd been to in the last days. She described with the pen the beach and the great, wild sweep of the bay itself.

She gave herself up to the process, her mug of coffee cooling next to her, the evening dimming at the window now that autumn wasn't far away. And with a free hand, not even resorting to the 'Letraset' she would have used back in college days, she wrote things onto it, including a name for the road between the village and the bay where trees arched towards each other. She called it 'the tunnel'. She was surprised to see how densely marked she made her map of this 'empty' place.

The phone rang about a week after her visit to Saint Trothan's. She answered it straight away.

'Maggie?'

It was Graham.

There was a small coughing noise. 'I thought you'd want to know,' Graham said uncertainly. 'They're having a sort of "service" for Trothan.'

Maggie's throat tightened at the sense of finality.

'They can't have a funeral, not without...'

'No,' Maggie said quickly.

There was a pause; then, 'You'll come, eh?'

'I can't, can I?' Maggie said. 'I'm not invited.'

'Yes,' Graham said. 'George asked me to ask you.'

Maggie hesitated, unsure whether to believe this.

'I'll pick you up. We can go together.'

A white buttoned blouse and a collar too tight. Maggie could only breathe in short sips. When she and Graham arrived in the doorway of the roofless church and saw the packed crowd in there, she stopped. Took a step back into Graham. He resisted, hands firm on her arms, gently propelling her. And then Nora saw her, stepped forward with an outstretched hand and a welcome.

Maggie stepped in to join the mourners lining the inside walls. Latticed sunlight and bird chatter poured in. She'd thought Nora and George might choose the beach. But Saint Trothan's enfolded them all amidst its ivy-scrabbled walls and allowed no one to be snubbed. Faces and eyes had to open onto each other. Maggie tried to keep her head high, to be an adult presence amongst these people who the wild running of her mind had told her were congregating against her. She stood shoulder to shoulder with them, Graham a buffer on one side.

Mobility Man was there, for once not in his fluorescents; a woman with hair the colour of Nora's, a slimmer version of her with a cluster of children; Audrey and another teacher released briefly from the school to pay their respects. Sally and Callum. And there were others Maggie half knew, half recognised.

Nora and George stood where the altar had presumably once been, puffed-up with a strain almost visible in George's too close shave which had left a rash and Nora's great breasts stretching a pale green dress at its bodice. Next to them stood a young blonde woman who with practised calm held a folder clasped loosely in her hands.

'You're going to go?' Carol had asked on the phone. 'You sure that's a good idea?'

'Why?'

'You've no obligation, have you?'

'Carol, I spent a lot of time with that child. It meant something.'

'I meant to his parents. They've not exactly made life easy for you, have they?'

Maggie hesitated. 'I'm not sure.'

'Really?'

'Whether I got it right.'

Carol had let out a great sigh then. 'Up to you. You'll be leaving that mess soon anyway, I guess.'

Once everyone had shuffled into place, almost giddy with the intimacy, the young blonde woman spread open the folder, looked over it at the circle of faces and began.

'Friends, we're here today because...'

Maggie's control was ripped from her. She bowed her head, felt Graham make an awkward grab at her wrist which he patted and then dropped. She rode the rest of the short service in an inner wrangle with tears and the broken beat of her breathing.

She forced away the young woman's words, listening instead for the echoes embedded in the stones, feeling the openness to the sky. No one would be able to hide anything here. Perhaps that was the point of a church; that all was revealed, to each other, to a god. She imagined a terrible explosion of truth blowing the roof clean off its rafters to leave the congregation staring at each other in sudden recognition as if the wind had stolen their clothes.

When she was calmer, she allowed in a little more of the speech until another nerve flared and the tide flooded again.

She pictured the saint in mute-coloured robes, a benign face and sandals; floating over the North Sea on a millstone. The image was clichéd but soothing.

'We are the ones who are left and naturally we are sad,' the voice said, quietly ringing between the walls. 'But let's concentrate for a few moments on our own special memories of Trothan. Let's send him on his crossing knowing that his mortal friends have not forgotten him.'

They were asked to join hands. She felt Graham's Scottish reserve bristling against this to her left. He looked at her quickly, sighed, then looked away as he snatched up her hand, holding it in his calloused one as he might the handle of a shovel. Everyone else uneasily obliged, turning side-on if necessary to allow the linking, shuffling their feet and avoiding eye contact. Maggie was pushed back, pushed *herself* back, out of the main circle into a corner, still hanging onto Graham's hand. But to her right a woman she didn't know looked over her shoulder and reached out to Maggie as if summoning a dance partner. An older woman with knotty knuckles and a gold ring on her wedding finger, smiling.

Maggie wiped her palm on her coat and stepped forward.

Seeing the bandage the woman said: 'Don't worry – I'll be gentle.'

Maggie felt the careful contact of the woman's warm, dry skin, and was suddenly reminded of her mother's hand. Walking to school on a summer's morning. The shuffling over, the circle stabilised; joining up the random fragments of Trothan's life. Despite the muddle of her pain Maggie felt a sudden lightening and looked up for a moment towards the sky and the branches that interlocked, parodying eaves. In between them the white spaces still spread above her. She breathed deeply.

'Hold on to him in your thoughts, talk of him often, repeat things he used to say. And let your love and regard show to Nora and to George.'

The walls hugged their backs, held Maggie in a moment of silent reflection, her head bowed now like the others. And into the midst of it something fell onto the grassy floor with a 'plop'. It was followed by a trumpeting call, keening from above. Maggie ducked, then shot a glance up. A huge white gull was heckling down at them from a perch on the church wall. It threw its head back, opened its bill and wailed.

'Bloody mawkies,' muttered Graham, leaning towards her to whisper. 'That's herring gulls to you by the way.'

Then the gull's cry broke up into raucous laughter before it glittered into creaky flight and abandoned its attempt at breaking open the shell. The shock broke the congregation into nervous laughter; hands were dropped, dissolving the tension of the circle. Audrey Thompson caught Maggie's eye and smirked.

Maggie and Graham joined the drift of people across the shadowy lawns to drive to the hotel for beer and sandwiches.

Once they'd joined the convoy for the short journey in Graham's car, he yanked open his collar and breathed out heavily. '"The crossing", what was that all about?'

'A mystery,' Maggie said. The image of the crossing seemed appropriate though; the boat, a journey of some kind, surely the sea.

'You know, Maggie, it is about time you spilt the kidneys.' Graham said.

'You what?'

'The beans, the beans,' Graham said.

There was a brief silence as they drove into the village back streets and found a place to park. He turned off the engine and neither moved.

'You're like an over-inflated beach ball. I was afraid you were going to explode in there.'

'Messy,' Maggie said.

'Aye. Beans, gases...'

Maggie stared ahead at the hotel wall. 'Okay,' she said.

TWENTY
TWO

Sitting opposite Maggie in his favourite Oxford restaurant, Richard raised a wine glass and she raised hers in reply.

'We did it,' he said. Must be the quickest turn-around in publishing history.'

They clinked glasses.

A copy of the West Africa Atlas lay next to her elbow on the restaurant table. She'd leafed through it very quickly in the meeting with the Head of Humanities and the Distribution Manager, but as ever, she wanted to check that her contributions had been reproduced well and that no corruptions or inaccuracies had crept into the captions since she checked the proofs.

She flicked through the pages now, let it lie open at her eccentric graphic about Lagos's growth, and pushed it slightly in Richard's direction, waiting to see if he would comment. He didn't.

'What did you think of this one?'

'Quite creative,' he said. 'Where did you get the idea?'

She looked down at the page. 'From a colleague.'

'Oh?'

His tone pulled her eyes back up.

'A cartographer up there I don't know about?' he said.

'I thought you might veto it.'

'You've made Lagos seem quite extraordinary.'

'It's a riddle of a place.' She tipped her head back, took another sip of the wine that unfurled a few more inner feathers as if to release her into flight. 'It's been intriguing me for a while now. Perhaps I'll go there, see if I can answer the riddle.'

'Are you serious?' He frowned slightly. 'Bit dangerous, isn't it?'

She tried to picture him in the sweat and scrum of Lagos, still wearing his chunky polo neck. She shrugged.

'Why did you think I'd veto your graphic?'

'A wee bit unconventional?' she said.

He smirked at her.

She stared back. 'What?'

He imitated her, 'a wee bit,' and then laughed. 'How's the Pacific going?'

She ducked her head. It was only early September, and because the deadline was the end of November it hadn't yet felt urgent, even though she knew there was weeks of work in it.

'It's on my list,' she said, taking a long sip of wine; floating now.

He grinned back at her.

'Nice wine,' she said. 'It's been a long time since I've been somewhere like this. Makes me feel like a grown-up.' She looked around at the Italian suavity of the restaurant. Headlights flashed in through the plate glass next to them and tyres sizzled faintly on the rainy street. People strode the pavement, catching at each other's umbrellas. Inside they were dry, warm, soothed by wine, smiled on by the kindly waiter who now delivered a plate of bruschetta to the table. Maggie breathed in the aroma of tomatoes, garlic, Mediterranean sun, and wriggled slightly in her seat.

'It's not quite like this up there,' she said, indicating the North with a backward nod of her head.

'No foodies?'

'Bag of salt and vinegar in the pub if you're lucky.'

She bit into the crisp bread, tasted the soft topping, fresh basil. She closed her eyes as she chewed and swallowed. When she opened her eyes, Richard was chewing without much obvious relish, smiling wryly at her.

He held her gaze. 'What about it, then?'

'About what?' She grabbed a second piece. 'Sorry about my manners. Can't help it. It's so delicious.' Her words were lost in the next bite, just as good.

'You must realise that Jean was asking you to apply,' Richard said.

She reached for a sprinkle of fresh parmesan, scattered it lavishly on the next piece. 'How many have you had?' Her third hovered near her mouth.

'It's fine,' he dabbed his mouth with the serviette. 'Your need is greater than mine, I think.'

There was another pause and then he prompted her again. 'So?'

'What?'

'Are you going to apply? Then you can be a Commissioning Editor like me, come back to Oxford and eat like Cleopatra every night.'

Her chewing slowed. He was leaning in slightly and she could smell something on him. Was it vanilla? He looked like one of those old TV adverts for pipe tobacco. Redolent of handsome homeliness.

'They obviously really want you,' he said.

'Can I bathe like she did too?'

'It's not ass's milk then, in the Pentland Firth?'

She circled the air with a finger as she swallowed another mouthful. 'Jellyfish,' she said. 'You don't get jellyfish in ass's milk, do you?'

He sat back in his seat as if satisfied, rubbed his hands together.

She was surprised how the thought of the place now, the sense of her great distance from it, brought a line of geese keening across a wide-open sky, and a surge from within as if she wished to rise skywards and join them.

She finished chewing.

Richard picked up the wine bottle, tipped it above her glass and raised an eyebrow in enquiry.

She got back on the train at Oxford and started the fifteen hour journey north, watching the old, familiar built-up places drop away and hours later recognising some of the towns she'd driven through six months before. Invergordon, Golspie, Brora. The trainline looped way inland across dark moorland, passing rowans brilliant with berries, and the shadows of deer flitting across bog before she regained the coast at Thurso and the top eastern corner of Britain.

She moved into the rented cottage Graham had helped her find, a little north-east of Dunnet Bay on the north side of the peninsula – a landowner he knew; a long lease. And she took her car to Murdo MacDonald in Quarrytown. He wiped oily hands on a rag after the MOT and declared the car 'not a bad wee banger' that would do her another year or two.

Geese arrowed in on their journeys south, waking her with their nightly choruses. She worked on the Pacific Atlas and made phone calls to Carol and Richard, even Helen sometimes. The frosts started and the occasional trees bronzed and then bared themselves; the moors rang out a burnished red with dying blaeberry bushes. The winds began again, merciless and cutting. On the sand-flats lugworms built their castles and birds arrived strutting from the Arctic – purple sandpiper and turnstone – bringing winter in their feathers.

With the shrinking days and the solstice, the great hinge of the year, her life contracted further to fireside, drawn curtains, the phone. A new work project and books. The dome of rising dough. It seemed a hibernation, almost an ending, curling up cat-like inside herself, protecting vital organs; her extremities no longer of concern.

But then in February there was suddenly light again, sharp and transparent, and the birds gathered such volume at dawn that she could no longer sleep through it. Graham came grinning to the door, saying Mary and he would be moving in nearby. Now he was going to be a father, the commute from Helmsdale was no longer practical. She visited them with a bottle of wine some evenings and Graham stopped smoking, even outside. The baby was due in June, he told her with a rare sparkle in his eyes. A midsummer bairn, he said, but not to go expecting a faery child or anything.

Hazel catkins dangled and sea thrift burst in miniature pink mountains all over the headlands. On some days there was warmth in the sun. Eggs would soon be laid. And when Maggie went to see the guillemots making ready on the cliffs at Dunnet Head, they seemed almost like old friends.

It was early April, not long after the return of the wheatear from Africa, the tiny bird whose 'chick-chack' made Maggie look up just in time to see a white flash of rump disappear over a dyke. She and her visitors were scrambling around on the rocks and crumbled wall that cut off the entrance to Ham Bay, making of it a tiny harbour. It was a sunny day and fresh enough to keep jumpers on. Great pillars of cloud were building over the Pentland Firth, frothy and white and stacked up so as to remind one of the height of the Earth's atmosphere. The green land around Dunnet Head was re-asserting itself out of winter's coarse yellow pallor.

Carol spread out a rug on the dry rocks and unpacked boiled eggs, slices of buttered bread, tomatoes, sausage rolls. She'd brought an enormous flask of tea which was strong and milky, searing with steam as she poured it into two mugs.

'Here.' She held out one to Maggie, who took it but continued to stand, looking out across the water with binoculars around her neck.

'Jamie. Fran,' Carol called the children who were crouched over a rock pool, poking something with a stick. Fran's blonde hair was still held in the two plaits Maggie had put in for her that morning.

'This is how I used to keep the wind from stealing my hair on a day like this,' she'd said, finishing each plait with the purple toggle Fran had insisted on.

The child had looked up at her, concerned, and said, 'Did the wind steal all your hair?'

'Only temporarily,' said Maggie.

'She used to have lovely long hair,' Carol said. 'Remember? When she used to come and stay with us?'

Fran frowned. 'Maybe.'

'I'm growing it a wee bit again,' Maggie said.

'Oh,' Fran had said.

'Do you two want orange juice?' Carol asked the children, taking out cardboard cartons. They lifted their heads from the pool and scampered over, barefoot, sitting cross-legged on the rug.

'Have you seen any yet?' Jamie asked Maggie. The bay was well known for its grey seal colony.

'Not yet. You have to be patient.'

'But what if they don't come today?'

Carol and the children would need to get packed, ready to leave first thing the next day.

'There's always the summer holidays when you'll come and visit me again.'

Jamie brightened.

She pointed out shags hanging their wings out to dry on one of the skerries where the bay's waist opened back out into the Pentland Firth. 'Scarfies,' she said, 'that's what they're called here.'

Each of the children looked at them through the binoculars.

Fran was looking at the clear water, turquoise-coloured where it washed in above the pale sand. 'Can we swim here?'

'No,' snapped Carol. 'Keep away from the water. It's very deep and dangerous.'

Maggie heard the implicit criticism. She shouldn't have brought the children here. A sandy beach would have been much more relaxing.

'I doubt you'd enjoy it,' said Maggie. 'It's not exactly warm. And...' She gathered her hands into claws and launched them at the children, snapping them open and shut. 'There's crabs,' she said as Jamie sniggered slightly and Fran squealed.

Maggie looked across the tiny bay, back inland. A high grassy bank on the far shore was always kept mown by the people of the house opposite; a good vantage point for watching wildlife. Maggie saw that someone was up on the path now, facing the sea. She looked at the figure through binoculars, starting from the feet and drawing her gaze upwards. As she half expected, the person's head was covered in close amber-blonde curls, and the woman stared down into the water of the bay. She'd seen little of Nora over the winter, or even since the memorial service for Trothan, probably because she'd moved further away from the village.

Fran tugged at Maggie's arm from behind her. She was looking in the opposite direction, pulling her towards something. 'Is that a dog in the water?'

'Look, there's two.' It was Jamie now, sounding excited.

'It's a young one. It's a young one. Oh, look, Auntie Maggie.'

Maggie swung around and saw two grey heads, one large, one smaller, risen on curious, long necks from the water. She saw their wide round eyes and flaring nostrils and put the binoculars in front of Fran's eyes, adjusting for size.

Carol was getting up from the rug now and Jamie clamouring for a shot with the binoculars.

'It turned and looked at me.' Fran jumped up and down. 'Mum. The seal looked at me.'

'Isn't that another one?' Carol pointed to the rocks and a large grey shape flopping its way awkwardly across boulders. It slipped into the sea, transforming itself, pouring like silk. It dived, showing a silent round of oily back before surfacing again alongside the other two. The seals made sudden, splashy dives and then rapidly resurfaced as if they'd been dancing underwater.

'Listen,' Maggie said.

They all strained in the direction she indicated towards a low platform of rocks at the base of a stack. And heard it. A longing, a melancholy call.

'Is he singing?' Fran threw her arms around Maggie's waist and looked up at her.

'Yes, love. He's singing,' and she played with the tail of Fran's plait as she gazed out to where the song came from.

Nora was still up on the path, listening and watching too. She and Maggie turned a little towards each other and Nora's free hand parted from her side, rose and opened slowly, into a high, wide wave. She held her hand there for several seconds, the fingers dark against the pale sky, parting wide so that light filled their negatives.

The sisters returned the wave, Maggie holding it for a little longer, opening her hand in the same way as if to meet and match the other woman's.

Acknowledgements

I'd like to thank Hamish Ashcroft for inspiring me with his astonishing map-drawing skills when he was six years old. Apologies to the people of Castletown and Dunnet Bay whose marvellous location and stories I've inhabited with invented characters.

For help with the development of the novel I'm grateful to the Scottish Book Trust's mentoring scheme and the support of Caitrin Armstrong, Jan Rutherford and my excellent mentor Andrew Crumey. Early readers Sarah Salway, Elspeth Mackay and Phil Horey gave me invaluable feedback, and my agent Jenny Brown has been steadfast in her encouragement and deserves a medal for patience. To my hosts and fellow writers at the Château de Lavigny writers' residence in September 2012 I owe the courage to press the 'send' button.

For technical advice on map history and map-making, thanks are due to Carolyn Anderson, and to Anne Mahon and Vaila Donnachie of HarperCollins Publishers, particularly the latter for her careful reading of a draft. For help on wildlife matters thanks go to Kenny Taylor, Highland Council Ranger Paul Castle, and Helen McLachlan of WWF Scotland. 'PC Pedro' knows who he is and was of great assistance as was Jane Bechtel, Humanist Celebrant. Any factual errors are my own.

To the good people of Freight Books – a grand salute for your belief in this work and for all your publishing skills. For her sensitive and creative editing, thanks go to Elizabeth Reeder.

Finally, of the many people who have encouraged me, the last mention must go to Gavin Wallace who was a wonderful supporter of writers and writing through his positions at the Scottish Arts Council and Creative Scotland and is greatly missed.